To Live and Die in Texas

American Blood
Apache Shadow
Apache Storm
Apache Strike
Battle of the Teton Basin
Christmas in the Lone Star State
Cutter's Reach
Falconer's Law
Flintlock
Gone to Texas
Green River Rendezvous
Gunmaster
Gunsmoke on the Sierra Line
High Country
Killer Gray
Lobo Riler
Mountain Courage
Mountain Honor
Mountain Massacre
Mountain Passage
Mountain Renegade
Mountain Vengeance
Promised Land
Revenge in Little Texas
Showdown at Seven Springs
Texas Blood Kill
Texas Bound

Texas Gundown
Texas Helltown
The Black Jacks
The Border Captains
The Fire-Eaters
The Long Hunters
The Marauders
The Outlaw Trail
The Town Killers
To Live and Die in Texas
Trail Town
War Lovers

As Hank Edwards
Bad Blood
Border War
Death Warrant
Gray Warrior
Gun Glory
Iron Road
Lady Outlaw
Lawless Land
Ride For Rimfire
River Raid
Steel Justice
The Judge
Thirteen Notches

As Dale Colter
Dead Man's Ride
Diablo at Daybreak

To Live and Die in Texas

Jason Manning

DEDICATION

To Ethan Ellenberg, my agent for the past thirty years.
Thank God.

CONTENTS

Chapter One

As Cord Colbry rode into Ellsworth, Kansas, and down the main street he marveled at how much the cow town had grown since his last visit, two summers before.

There were a lot more people and a great many new buildings and he couldn't help but stare at both. Ellsworth hadn't even existed a few years ago and now it was thriving. Proof of this was a long, white, three-story clapboard with the name Drovers Cottage emblazoned across the front in letters as tall as a grown man. He figured at least fifty men could line up shoulder to shoulder on the covered porch that stretched across the front of the building, and was pretty sure he had not seen a bigger structure in his whole life.

Colbry was an average-sized man, closing in on forty years of age, all grit and bone, broad in the shoulders and lean in the flanks. There was little to distinguish him from the hundreds of other cowboys who had or would visit the cowtown this summer. He had piercing sky-blue eyes that glittered like ice in a creased, square-jawed face bronzed by constant exposure to the elements. He wore a shirt of oft-mended, sun-faded blue cotton twill tucked into brown canvas pants which were in turn stuffed into black stovepipe boots, all covered with a patina of dust. A Smith and Wesson .45 Schofield rode butt-forward in a holster on his left hip. A converted 50-70 Sharps rifle was snug in a saddle scabbard under his right leg.

He was gawking so intently at the hostelry that he didn't notice his leggy buckskin horse was veering into the path of an oncoming buckboard. Boots had a will of his own and sometimes exercised it. In this case he was determined to get to the nearest water trough and Colbry had to struggle to hinder him from getting what he wanted. But this time he wasn't trying to. He was still gawking at the buildings and busy boardwalks and didn't pay much attention to a wagon coming down the street in the opposite direction. The wagon's driver shouted, "Damn it, mister! Watch where you're going!" and sawed at the reins, trying to stop the mules in the wagon's traces. Mules were hard to get moving but harder still to stop.

Colbry sharply checked his thirsty horse, leaning back in the saddle, knuckles white and arm muscles bulging, and it was enough to slow Boots down long enough for the buckboard to block the horse from the trough. The buckskin snorted and shied away from the mules as the nearest one put its ears back and snapped at him.

The buckboard driver was a young man in a dusty black suit. He was slender, with a trimmed black beard, a sallow complexion burned by the summer sun, eyes dark and a sour expression on his face. Beside him sat a pretty young lady in what could have been her Sunday-go-to-meeting dress, a reticule decorated with ribbons and lace in her lap, and a matching parasol tilted over a shoulder to keep the blistering summer sun off the back of her alabaster neck. She wore a gray dress with lace on the sleeves, the collar and the hem, and at least a dozen dainty white buttons down the front. Her golden curls were done up under a matching bonnet but long strands had escaped here and there. Having not seen a woman in about two months, Colbry couldn't help but stare. That seemed to make the woman self-conscious, and it also put a dark scowl on her companion's face.

"You must be from Texas, Sir," sneered the man, after finally succeeding in stopping the buckboard. His tone of voice made plain that he harbored a measure of contempt for anything Texan and that he fully intended his comment to be considered an insult. "Only a Texan would be so ignorant as to cut in front of a team of mules."

The young lady smiled softly, a smile Colbry took to be a somewhat embarrassed apology for the man's rudeness. She didn't seem to mind his staring at all. He dragged his gaze away from her and looked instead at the dark scowl on the face of the man beside her.

"Sorry about that," he said, with a wry smile that made plain he wasn't exactly filled with remorse.

"And I would thank you not to gape at my wife."

Colbry nodded. He realized he had been looking at her more than he probably should have. "It's just that I don't think I've ever seen such beauty in all my years." He was still smiling, but the smile didn't reach his eyes when he turned them on the man who had spoken. He turned his horse alongside the buckboard so as not to hinder the traffic of other people on the street—people in wagons, on horseback and on foot—then leaned forward in his saddle and draped his arms across the saddle horn. "It's true I was lucky enough to be born in Texas," he drawled. "Now I understand why some residents of this town aren't fond of Texas cowboys, even when their livelihood depends on us. But it seems to me you should be proud that other men admire your wife. You must be quite an hombre to warrant such a catch."

The man in the buckboard was taken aback by Colbry's compliment, not to mention his lengthy and literate discourse, but was quick to resume his expression of angry disdain. His tone made it obvious that as far as he was concerned Texas cowboys ranked somewhere near the top of his list of creatures worthy of contempt. "Only a Texas cowboy would stare at a young lady in that manner, sir."

"There's no fooling you, is there?" drawled Colbry. "I am a cowboy and I've spent more than a couple of months eating the dust of almost a thousand head of ornery longhorns on the Chisholm Trail." He decided that the man must be insecure and defensive, threatened by all the young, strapping cowpokes that swarmed a cattle town in the summer months, but he couldn't resist goading the man by continuing to gaze at the woman while he spoke. "I must say, ma'am, you are prettier than a sunrise."

She blushed at the compliment.

"It is not fitting to comment so regarding another man's wife," snapped the man. "I would have your name, sir."

"Cord Colbry. And your handle?"

"My name is Luther Keyes. I am an investor and a businessman and I am here on business."

"So am I. Well, here on business anyway. An investor and a businessman, you say.. Well, that sounds mighty important."

Keyes made a sweeping gesture. "Look around you, sir. New enterprises are springing up all around this town. My goal is to assist in making Ellsworth the greatest entrepot on the plains."

"Entrepot?"

Keyes snorted disdainfully. "Forgive me. For a moment I forgot to whom I was speaking. An entrepot is a center of trade and commerce. Understandably, many want to realize their dream of being a part of this grand opportunity but lack adequate funds to do so. I provide the funding."

"And what do you get out of it?'

"I charge a fair amount of interest on my loans and offer generous terms for repayment."

The woman spoke up. "Luther inherited some money when our father died. He has been … helping people ever since."

Colbry nodded, noting her hesitation as she picked her words carefully. "Well, isn't that something," he drawled.

"As you can imagine, I am a busy man, sir," said Keyes. "But before we go, I think you owe my wife an apology."

Colbry sat in his saddle for a moment, looking bemused, a wry smile still nestling at the corners of his mouth. It was the mask he wore when he was perturbed. He wasn't sure why he needed to apologize for complimenting a pretty woman, even a married one, but he had to concede that most of the women he knew personally weren't ladies. So he tried to look penitent and touched the brim of his battered, sweat-stained hat.

"Sorry if I offended you, ma'am."

"Consider that your first lesson in manners," said Keyes, and was about to whip the team into motion when Mrs. Keyes put a hand on her husband's arm.

"Thank you, but you needn't worry. didn't offend me," she told Colbry, then tilted her head curiously. "That's a magnificent horse you have."

"Sure is. Strong and durable. Fast, too. I've had him since he was a colt. He's been chasing cows, mustangs and Apaches ever since." He glanced at the mules in the buckboard's leathers. "Once upon a time, before Boots here, I rode a mule."

Mrs. Keyes looked amused. "A cowboy on a mule? I think perhaps you are pulling my leg, sir."

"Not at all. I wasn't pushing cows then. I was in the army, further west. Apacheria. Mules may not be as fast, but in

Apacheria, which is a hard country, they are sturdy enough to get you where you're going."

"But not as quickly as that magnificent beast you ride, I would guess."

"True words. But one time I did see a mule beat a horse in a race. It was up Colorado way a few years back. It was a mile-long run down a dry wash that circled part way around a mountain. The mule was up against a Kentucky-bred mare that had already won a passel of races. But the mule bested her. You see, the mare ran around that mountain. The mule ran up one side of it and down the other."

Delighted, the lady clapped her gloved hands and laughed softly. "But I've heard that mules can be bad-tempered. Is that not so?"

Colbry had the feeling that Mrs. Keyes was prolonging the conversation just to annoy her husband. Or maybe she liked his company. But Colbry was humble enough to think that unlikely. "They can be if you treat them poorly. They're pretty fearless, too. I saw a mule kill a cougar years ago. Boots here has made a hobby of killing snakes, and once he scared off a cougar stalking my night camp in the Organ Mountains."

"Oregon? You have traveled widely, sir."

"I have, ma'am. but not as far as Oregon. La Sierra de los Organos are mountains in the New Mexico Territory."

"Oh, I see. Well, your handsome horse is a very brave fellow, then," said Mrs. Keyes.

Her scowling husband finally spoke up. "We must be on our way, dear," he said gruffly and, with one final glower at Colbry, stirred up the mules and drove on down the street.

Colbry let Boots drink his fill at the water trough as he watched the buckboard roll away, Colbry envied Luther Keyes. Not because the man had money and owned a business but because he had a polite and very pretty woman for a wife. It made him reflect on his own life, particularly what he had accomplished in the years since the end of the war between the states, and the fact that all he owned in the world was a horse, a rifle, an old saddle, a pistol, and a handful of silver dollars. Truth was, he had never had an opportunity to marry a proper young lady, to put down roots and raise a family. In fact, he had never owned the ground he slept on.

Boots was done at the trough when the shrill sound of a steam whistle came from the other end of town and fiddle-footed a little. Colbry caught a glimpse of the Kansas Pacific train rolling in from the east, visible at the north end of the street, the thick plume of black smoke billowing out of the mogul's smokestack like a backward question mark against the pale blue sky. The whistle reminded him that he was here on a job, and he tried to chase all the 'what ifs' out of his mind as he heeled Boots into motion up the street. He counted five saloons on his way to the town sheriff's office. That was two more than he had seen on his first visit to Ellsworth the previous summer. You could tell how well a town thrived on the frontier by the number of watering holes it had.

It was customary for a trail boss to check in with the local law to acquaint himself with the ordinances that would apply to a crew of rowdy cowboys soon to be visiting the town. In this case, Colbry had an additional motive. He wrestled the mule away from the trough and rode on up the street to the sheriff's office. He tied the buckskin to a hitching post and went inside. He smiled at the familiar face of the man who sat behind a cluttered kneehole desk to his right. Chancey Whitman was scribbling in a ledger and looked every bit as miserable as a man with a toothache.

But when he glanced up and saw Colbry his grimace turned into a friendly smile and he got to his feet, extending a hand across the desk.

"Cordell Colbry, as I live and breathe! Good to see you!"

Closing the door behind him and moving to the desk to take the sheriff's hand, Colbry shook it enthusiastically. "How have you been, Chancey?"

They had met the summer before, when Colbry had been just another cowpuncher riding for the Rocking Chair brand. He had come to Whitman's attention in a crowded saloon when the town sheriff was attempting to arrest a drunken cowboy who had lost his bankroll at poker and then declared the game rigged and drew his pistol on the badgetoter. Colbry had been sitting in on the game and, closer to the would-be-shooter than Whitman, had pistol-whipped the drunk before he could trigger his hogleg. He knew it in all likelihood neither man would walk away from a point-blank shootout as healthy as he had walked into it, but his hope was to make sure neither one ended up residing in boot hill.

"Can't complain," said the lawman. "I'm guessing you've come up with a herd like last time?" Whitman was a stocky man of medium height, his thick brown hair and bushy eyebrows generously sprinkled with gray. His face was brown and scarred like old saddle leather. His nose had been broken several times and looked it.

"That's right. If you're busy I can come back later."

Whitman glanced down at the ledger and his grimace returned. "Hell no. I'm more than happy to put this off 'til later. Got to keep a record of every feller I throw in a cell, you know." He tilted his head in the direction of the door to the cellblock. "So many of 'em these days I can't keep it straight in my own mind. Given my druthers, I'd rather be doing my rounds. Or chewing the fat with a friend. Never been partial to paperwork."

The sheriff gestured at the chair in front of the desk, indicating that Colbry was welcome to have a seat, and with a grunt settled back into his own. He was still talking. "Once the KP built a railhead here folks started pouring in. Last year they shipped more beef out of Ellsworth than Abilene ever did, and I believe the same will be true this year. So I'm getting to bust a lot of cowboy heads."

"Well, Abilene got too big and too tame, I guess. You had something to do with that, Chancey." Colbry settled back in the chair and smiled, knowing his friend wouldn't be able to resist the chance to talk about the highlights of his badge-toting career.

Whitman nodded. "Yep. Worked for the first city marshal, Tom Smith, and killed my first man in the Alamo Saloon on Cedar Street. That was quite a watering hole, Cordell. Even had an orchestra that played three times a day." He chuckled, shaking his head. "Not sure those cow punchers getting drunk on tanglefoot much appreciated that orchestra though. Smith was quite a character. He didn't use a gun to enforce the law. Just his fists. I think now I understand why. Cowboys go to a lot of trouble to learn gun-handling and some are quick draws. But they would hesitate to draw down on an unarmed man. Killing a lawman would have meant the hangman's noose. Now that I think about it, I reckon Smith was counting on that. Me, I wouldn't have had the nerve to do it the way he did. Met Wes Hardin, Ben Thompson, the Clement boys, cold killers all, over in Abilene."

Colbry nodded. "Can't say I've met any of those men and I'm mighty glad of that."

"Then the city trustees passed an ordinance that required the cowboys to check their guns when they came to town. More and more 'good citizens' had made Abilene their home and some started businesses. And after that they hired Wild Bill Hickok as marshal, Abilene was tamed and the citizens didn't want or need rowdy cowboys anymore. So when the railroad came here, so did the cowboys. And so did I."

"Guess that explains the big hotel down the street."

"That thing was built in Abilene by Joseph McCoy, you know. He sold it to a feller named Gore who sold it to another feller named McGeorge. Then it was torn down and McGeorge came here and put it up again, bigger and better than ever. Brought most of the lumber and such with him. Place has room for over a hundred guests. Has its own stable and carriage house, too." Whitney opened a drawer of his kneehole desk and pulled out a bottle of rye whiskey and two shot glasses. "Guess Ellsworth will be civilized soon, too. Reckon that then I'll have to move on again."

"How come?"

"Too many people means too much politics. I like to keep it simple. You break the law, I break you. Care to wet your whistle?" It was a rhetorical question so he was pouring the whiskey into the second glass while he said it.

Colbry leaned forward, picked up one of the shot glasses and knocked back the contents. The whiskey made him gasp, burning like liquid fire in his parched throat. He put the empty glass on the table and sat back in the chair, smiling gratefully at the rush of warmth inside that seemed to ease the aches and pains of a long trail.

"I seem to remember you rode for the Rocking Chair brand last summer," said Whitman, picking up the other glass. "Do you still?'

Colbry nodded. "John Ruston talked me into taking over as trail boss. Seems the man who had the job before me was dabbling in some brand burning of his own. Ruston stretched his neck. Last time I noticed, the feller's bones are still decorating an old pecan tree."

Whitman nodded. "Maybe that will scare off some of the rustlers. Depends on how desperate they are. But men who break the law often don't think they'll be the ones to get caught."

"Anyway, the boss stayed behind this time and kept his foreman with him, so I ended up with the herd."

"I met John Ruston some years ago in Abilene," reminisced Whitman, "when he came up with his herd. A good man. I reckon you wouldn't have worked for him had he not been."

Cord shrugged. "I've worked for men who weren't so good. But yes, he is. Tough as they come, but fair-minded. Never told a man to do a job he wasn't willing to do himself."

Whitman finished off his drink, sighed, and put the glass down to open another desk drawer and pull out a telegram which he placed on the desk with a sigh. "You'd best read that, amigo."

Colbry leaned forward. put the empty glass on the desk and picked up the telegram. As he read it his face became a stoic, sun-bronzed mask.

To the law in Ellsworth. Inform Rocking Chair trail boss. John Ruston dead. Sell herd. Return with all proceeds. B. Mackey, Sheriff, Lampasas.

Colbry read it twice, then slowly folded the telegram and sat there, silently rubbing his stubbled chin, staring at the folded telegram with a bleak expression on his face.

Whitman uncorked the whiskey bottle and refilled Colbry's glass. "Sorry to be the bearer of bad news, Cordell."

Colbry shook his head and muttered, "Damn it all. When did you get this?"

"About four weeks ago." Whitney drank his whiskey then refilled both glasses. "You were probably down in the Red River country about then. Have another drink."

Knocking back the second dose of bravemaker, Colbry stood up, again put the empty glass on the sheriff's desk and said, "Thanks, Chancey. Good to see you. I better go find a buyer for the herd."

"Sit down, son. I have more news for you."

Colbry sagged back into the chair and took a deep breath. He had done all kinds of work in his years of wondering after the war. Had worked for many bosses. But John Ruston's death hit him hard. The rancher had made him feel as though the Rocking Chair spread was his home, a feeling he had never experienced in any border town, army bivouac or mining camp. He had started out as a line rider, living on the boundaries of the ranch, rarely seeing the boss or the other hands. But then Ruston had named him trail boss, a position of great responsibility, and the cattleman's faith in him had meant a lot and had him thinking that maybe he could actually put down roots for the first time in his life. Now, that prospect was gone.

"John Ruston's daughter arrived in town a few days ago. Seems like someone knew where to send a telegraph to her, maybe Mackey, because she knew the Rocking Chair herd were headed this way." Whitman shrugged. "She's staying at that big hotel you saw on your way in." The sheriff stood up and came around the desk, leaning on the front edge and folding his arms across his chest. "You did know he had a daughter, didn't you?"

Colbry nodded. "He had two sons and a daughter. Both sons died some time ago and he sent her back east to live with his sister so she could become a proper lady and, I reckon, have an easier and better life than a woman could find on the open range. I think her name is Laura?"

"Laurie is what she told me. Sometimes I wish I had a family, then I think about all the things that can kill a person out here." Whitman shrugged and changed the subject. "Don't mean to tell you your business, but if I was you I'd see a feller named Orville Paxton. He's a cattle buyer and drives a hard bargain, but from what I've heard he's an honest man. My hunch is that you'll get the best price for Miss Ruston's cattle from him."

Colbry nodded, stood up and turned to the door.

"If you're still in town at sundown we could have supper at the Drovers Cottage," suggested Whitman. "Best grub in town. I'll pay."

Stunned by the news about John Ruston, Colbry said nothing but nodded again. Ordinarily he would sell the herd, pay off the trail drivers and then come back to town with the crew to keep them out of Whitman's crowded jail – or try to, anyway. And after a day or two of letting the Rocking Horse crew paint the town red – and having a little fun himself – he would collect them and lead the way back to Texas. But now his future was uncertain. He turned to leave the office.

"One more thing, Cordell," said Whitman. "They say Ellsworth is the most wicked cowtown of them all, and I believe that to be true. A lot of rowdy cowboys, and you know how they can be when they cut loose. But also our share of gamblers, confidence men, cutthroat thieves and whores. Seems like hardly a week goes by we don't have at least one shooting. All this by way of saying you need to watch your back. I know you're one tough hombre but, well, you're not the only tough hombre out there." The badgetoter rubbed his chin thoughtfully. "I'd say there are at least a dozen men in town—and more than few women too—who wouldn't shy away from murdering you without hesitation or remorse if they find out you're carrying the proceeds from the sale of a herd."

"Thanks for the warning." Colbry extended a hand.

Whitman nodded, shook the offered hand and wished him good fortune.

Chapter Two

Closing the door of the sheriff's office behind him, Colbry stood on the boardwalk a moment, watching the to-and-fro of the people on the wide dusty street, watching without really seeing. He was thinking about John Ruston, a man as big and tough as Texas itself, a man who lived life on his own terms. The kind that had known a lot of adversity and overcome it all. He realized he had fallen into the trap of thinking that nothing would bring Ruston down. It was a sobering reminder that death could come for anyone at any moment.

Hankering for another drink or two, he scanned the array of "watering holes" along this section of street. Then he looked at the telegram in his hand. The way he saw it, he had one last job to do for John Ruston and he needed to get it done. Sell the herd, locate Laurie Ruston, give her the money and find out if he still had a job. He even thought about letting her do the bartering with Paxton. But did she even know what a steer was worth? Maybe Paxton would take advantage of her. Even the most honest of battle buyers would try to get the best deal. Colbry shook his head and decided to sell the herd himself. Going to his tethered buckskin, he opened up one of the saddle bags and pulled out a folded envelope. Then he bent his steps north, toward the railroad track and the cattle pens adjacent to it.

Seeing just how many pens there were and how many hundreds of cattle were in them made Colbry stop dead in his tracks and stare. The pens were north of the iron road and stretched westward from the train station into a dusty haze raised by thousands of hooves. Off in the distance, a herd was being moved closer across the sun-seared grassy plain. About twenty stock cars were attached to a mogul parked alongside a water tower, chuffing thick balls of black smoke from its stack.

He was pleasantly surprised when it turned out that Orville Paxton wasn't hard to find. It seemed the cattle buyers used the train station to conduct their business and talk their trade amongst themselves. All he had to do was ask the station master to point the man out. Paxton was a tall, slender, elderly gentleman in a dusty burgundy coat and tan trousers. There was a white John Bull hat on his head. He greeted Colbry with an amiable smile and a robust handshake.

"Rocking Chair," mused Paxton. "John Ruston's brand. I met him in '67 over in Abilene. That first year we shipped about twenty thousand head of cattle back east. It was something to behold. Met him again in '69. Good man. How is he doing?"

"Not too good. I just found out he's dead."

The smile disappeared from the buyer's face. "I am damn sorry to hear that. How did it happen?"

Colbry shook his head. "No idea."

"What happens to the brand?"

"He had a daughter. I reckon she'd want the herd sold."

"I would be honored to meet her."

"She lives back east." Colbry figured it was up to Laurie Ruston herself how many people in Ellsworth knew about her presence.

"Well I am glad you sought me out, Mister…?"

"Colbry."

Paxton tilted his head curiously. "You're the trail boss?"

Colbry nodded and took a folded envelope out of a pocket, removed the wax-sealed letter it contained, and showed it to Paxton. The letter, written by John Ruston, identified him as the Rocking Chair trail boss, and by so doing, vouched for him to negotiate the sale of the herd. Paxton read the letter, nodded, and handed it back.

"Good enough. Well, sir, I am prepared to give you two dollars and a half for every head you pushed up here."

Colbry smiled faintly. He didn't hold it against Paxton for trying to low-ball him. "I'm thinking I have to get three dollars."

Paxton made a sweeping gesture in the direction of the cattle pens. "We have already seen more beeves this year than the whole of last year, and it's only the middle of the season yet."

Colbry nodded and extended a hand. Paxton grinned and took it, clearly thinking they were about to strike a deal—until Colbry said, "Good to meet you, Mr. Paxton, but I think I'll look for better offer from somebody else."

He started to pull his hand free but Paxton's grip tightened. The buyer's grin had vanished. "Very well, sir, three dollars per. When you bring them to the railhead, and we run them through for the final count, I will pay you."

"Good doing business with you," said Colbry. "I'll get the herd up here by sundown."

Returning to the street, he walked in the direction of the sheriff's office and untethered his horse then angled across the street, making for a saloon called the White Elephant. It occurred to him that a good employee would make meeting the boss his first priority, but he had been thinking about a shot of whiskey for several days now. The next time he came to town he would wind up with the payment for the herd, a sum of money only a fool would carry into a saloon. And, besides, he was a little nervous about meeting Laurie Ruston and was putting it off as long as possible.

He was about to secure Boots to the crowded hitching post in front of the saloon when he heard a woman call his name. He recognized the voice and glanced over his shoulder to see Mrs. Keyes emerging from the shade of an alley. She held her dress hem up just a bit with one hand to keep it from dragging on the dusty boardwalk in front of the White Elephant, her reticule clutched in the other. Colbry noticed that she no longer had her parasol. She stopped on the steps in front of him.

"Well I'll be," he drawled as he quickly scanned the street, wondering where Luther Keyes was, and then touched the brim of his sweat-ringed hat as he fastened his gaze on her. "Where's your husband, ma'am?" He couldn't resist letting his gaze stray to her narrow waist.

"Oh, he's in there." She said, dismissively, gesturing at the saloon's entrance, a pair of wooden doors with the establishment's name etched into the two glass panels in the center. "Five card stud is the love of his life. He's a very good player." The inflection in her voice as she spoke those last two words gave Colbry the impression that she considered poker a serious rival for her husband's attention. "He likes for me to be by his side while he plays. Says I distract the other men at the table." This was accompanied by a shrug of genuine indifference. "But after a while all the talk and the smoke and the loud piano playing gets to me." She smiled faintly and he could tell she wasn't in a smiling mood.. "So I was just out here for some fresh air. I saw you and, um, I wanted to apologize for Luther's rudeness earlier. My given name is Mary, by the way,"

"Thanks." Colbry was about to add that he figured she often had to apology for her husband's manner, but decided against it. I would advise you not to stand outside of a saloon, Mary. You might be mistaken for a two-dollar whore."

She smiled sadly. "I sometimes feel like one."

He didn't respond to that and, instead, said, "I think your husband is a fool if he puts anything before you. You're as pretty as a diamond flush. Surprised he even lets you out of his sight." He looked around again. "Especially in a town like this."

The compliment brought a grateful smile to her lips, a brief respite from the anxiety revealed by her furtive eyes as she kept glancing this way and that. "Yes, yes he is. Awfully possessive. I…I need to tell you something. Could we talk privately?" She didn't wait for an answer, grabbing his wrist and pulling him toward the mouth of the alley. He brought Boots along with him.

Colbry could have freed himself easily but curiosity got the better of him and he let her drag him along. The alley between the saloon and an adjacent clapboard building was cluttered with wind-blown trash, a couple of trapped tumbleweeds, and a few empty barrels. The sun was high in the brass-colored sky now, and there was just enough shade to provide a respite from the burning heat of a summer day. She turned and Cord was startled to see tears glistening in her eyes.

"Please!," she whispered. "You have to help me!"

"Help you with what, ma'am?"

"Help me get away from Luther. I…I have a confession to make. I am not his wife. I'm his sister. Even so, he is horribly jealous. And…and he can be violent. I can't tell you all the terrible things he has done to me. And I have never given him cause to do such things!"

"Is that so." Colbry wasn't sure he wanted to know the details of the "terrible things" or that he was even buying her story. But he tried to keep the skepticism out of his tone. "Why don't you tell that to the law?"

"I can't! Luther said he would punish me if I said anything to anyone!" She glanced beyond him, raising a trembling hand to arrest the progress of a tear running down her cheek. "He can be … very cruel. He can be a violent man when his temper gets the best of him. But, well, I have a feeling you're my only hope. Please! I beg you! I'll … I'll do anything. Just help me. please!" She stepped into him, wrapping her arms around him and pressing her face against his chest to muffle her sobs.

Out of the corner of his eye Colbry saw Luther Keyes coming around the back corner of the saloon. He wasn't surprised. Dropping the buckskin's reins, he grabbed Mrs. Keye's arm as he turned to face the other man, turning her as well and keeping her in front of him. She stumbled, and the reticule she held fell to the ground. Colbry didn't let go, his arm locked around her waist now. His grip tightened until she gasped in pain and he pulled her up tight against him. Even so, Keyes brought his pistol to bear, arm extended, aiming right at Colbry's head. His hand was steady, his eyes as dead as the grave. Colbry had a hunch Keyes had killed before and would do so again without hesitation.

"Let her go!" snapped Keyes, still moving until he was deeper into the alley and had his back to the wall of the building adjacent to the White Elephant. "Do it or I'll put a bullet right between your eyes."

Colbry's eyes were like blue ice and his expression was as hard as stone. "So you're in a hurry to meet the hangman."

"Who would blame me for protecting the honor of my wife?"

Colbry almost called him on his claim that Mary was his wife, but decided that at this point it wouldn't do anybody any good. "Well, I reckon you could shoot me," acknowledged Colbry. "But before I died I might trigger this gun that's poking her in the back."

Mary Keyes had gone pale and she trembled while throwing a terrified glance at her accomplice. "For God's sake, Luther!" she shouted. "Lower that gun! Can't you tell that he means it?"

"He's bluffing, Mary! He won't shoot you."

Mary Keyes looked around and up into Colbry's cold steel-blue eyes and looked quite afraid of what she saw in them. "The hell he won't!" she hissed. "For God's sake, lower that gun!"

Colbry shifted the woman he held tightly a little to his left, just enough for Keyes to see that his holster was empty.

Boots began stomping and whickering. The buckskin hadn't moved much after Colbry had dropped the reins, but he acted like he considered Keyes a threat and was on the verge of rearing. Luther looked warily at the big horse and slid sideways along the wall, Cord knew this was the deciding moment. What happened next was up to the other man. Maybe Luther Keyes didn't give a damn about the woman. Or maybe he was smart enough to know that Colbry was right, that gunning down a man in a cowtown probably meant he would end up with a rope around his neck unless he managed to flee Ellsworth and elude the posse that would go after him. But it had been Colbry's experience that a lot of people acted irrationally in a dangerous situation, so he was ready for whatever happened.

There was no emotion in Colbry at that moment. He had no intention of shooting the woman and thought he had a fair chance of getting the best of the other man. There was nothing more to think about. Confronted by the very real possibility that he could be killed, he would not hesitate to kill first. A profound calm had come over him. It had always been that way when he found himself in a dangerous situation. He had no idea why.

Luther met his gaze and then drew a long sigh and relaxed. He was convinced that his accomplice would die if he pulled the trigger, and maybe he would, too. In the past, his victims had been too scared to do anything but comply. But that wasn't the case this time and he wasn't prepared for that.

"You bastard," he said, resentfully, then lowered the Navy Colt and tossed it onto the ground between himself and Colbry. Arms away from his sides, his palms turned in Cord's direction, he muttered. "Just don't shoot her."

Colbry marched Mary across the alley, holding her up when she stumbled. As he pushed her into Luther he kicked the man's Navy Colt down the alley a good ten feet. Then he backed up and moved to the right, murmuring, "Ho-shuh, ho-shuh." Boots responded to the Apache horse talk and immediately quieted. Colbry grabbed the reins and used the Schofield still in his grip to motion for Luther and Mary to precede him to the mouth of the alley. Before they got there Chancey Whitman showed up, blocking the way.

"What's going on here?" growled the sheriff. When he recognized Colbry he said, "Your horse is a noisy feller. Heard him all the way across the street. Looked out the window in time to see you coming into this alley with..." he glanced at Mary skeptically, "...this lady here."

"He can be, when he's riled," allowed Colbry.

Whitman took stock of the situation, reading the expressions on the faces of all those present, then drew his pistol and pointed it at the couple. "You can put that pistola away, Cordell. Ain't never seen you shoot, but my guess is you only shoot to kill. And you don't want to do that."

"You're right. I don't."

Whitman nodded, having expected Colbry's response. "You have more important things to do. Pick up that feller's gun, will you? Might fall into the hands of a drunk or a kid. Then we'll all mosey on over to my office and have ourselves a talk."

Whitman led the way and Colbry brought up the rear, pausing to hitch his horse. When he entered the jail, Mary was seated in the chair facing Whitman's desk. Luther stood beside her, arms held out to the side while Whitman frisked him. Going to the sheriff's desk, Colbry unloaded Keyes' Navy Colt and put the pistol on the desk and the six bullets next to it. Then he went around the desk and opened the drawer and helped himself to a glass of the sheriff's whiskey. He was feeling edgy, now. It always happened that way. When there was danger his nervous system seemed to shut down. When the danger had passed it came roaring back to life. The whiskey helped smooth frayed nerves.

Whitman spun Luther around to face him. "I've seen you around. What's your handle?"

"Why that's Luther Keyes," said Colbry wryly, when Keyes hesitated. "He's a businessman and investor, or so I've been told. Didn't you know?" He looked at Mary, and debated whether to reveal that she was not a bride but a sister. He ended up deciding to sidestep that decision altogether. "And the little lady is for sure his partner in crime."

"You don't say." Whitney's tone of voice made clear he was being sarcastic. He glowered at Luther. "What are you up to in my town? By the way, mister, you really do not want to lie to me."

Luther sighed. "Mary is my sister, not my wife." He glared sullenly at Colbry. "We were going to rob that man there. Took him for a trail boss. Saw him head down to the cattle pens. I assumed he had sold his herd and had a good sum of money on him."

Whitman stood with arms folded, slowly shaking his head as he listened. "I take it you're new at this," he remarked drily. "Now empty your pockets and put everything on that desk. Move slow. I'm the nervous sort."

Luther Keyes obeyed and at the sheriff's request dejectedly filled in the details. He and his sister had arrived by train the day before yesterday, on the run from the law in St. Louis. They had fallen on hard times, lost their house to creditors, and had resorted to skullduggery, with Mary luring a man into a hotel room, Luther slipping in later while the man was grunting and thrusting on top of her, knocking the man out and robbing him of everything he had of value—money, gold watch and even boots. Their victim hadn't laid eyes on him and he had fled the scene while Mary ran down to the lobby, acting quite hysterical. She had convinced the authorities that she was just an innocent bystander. Fleeing westward, they had done the same thing in a couple of other towns and had marked Colbry as their next victim.

Hearing this, Colbry looked with surprise at Mary. "And here I thought you were a lady," he said, wearing a smile that had no humor in it.

She looked down. "Would you really have shot me?" she asked.

"Nope. Haven't shot a woman yet and don't plan to. But your brother might have if he managed to get off a shot after I put a bullet in his chest. But not me. There are too few pretty ladies in these parts to go around killing them."

Mary smiled faintly. "Would you have gone to bed with me if you hadn't seen me with Luther?"

Colbry shrugged. Asking himself the same question, he decided that in all likelihood he would have. He looked at Luther. "You, on the other hand, you would've been standing at the pearly gates had you not dropped that barking iron of yours."

Luther bristled at Colbry's assumption that he would have lost if it had come down to a shootout. But he just nodded sullenly and didn't say a word.

"You want to press charges, Cordell?" asked Whitman.

Colbry had already thought it over. He shook his head. "I've got to get back to Texas, and I reckon the local judge is pretty busy."

"True words. I figure it could be a few days, maybe longer, before the trial came up." Whitman tilted his head at the heavy door that led to the cellblock. "Most of those boys back there are cowpokes who will likely be fined and sent on their way. But some vandalism, a couple of assaults, four attempted robberies and an attempted murder are on the docket ahead of these two."

Colbry gave Luther and Mary Keyes one more look and shook his head again. "Doesn't sound like a place for a woman."

Whitman strolled around his desk and sat down behind it, frowning at the two would-be-robbers. He nodded at Luther. "I'll hold him and send some telegraphs down the rail line, see if he's wanted for anything serious elsewhere." His flinty gaze moved to Mary. "As for you, young lady, don't you dare leave town until I say you can. I will track you down and drag you back by the heels. I assume you have a hotel room here in town."

Mary nodded and in a small voice said, "Thank you, Sheriff."

As she turned to go, Colbry stepped aside and out of her way. Mary glanced sidelong at him with a faint and grateful smile. It appeared to him that she didn't seem overly concerned that her brother was going to be locked up.

When he turned to follow her across the threshold, Whitney called out a "Good luck, Cordell. And don't forget what I told you, Miss Ruston." Colbry lifted a hand, a parting gesture, as he stepped outside into the hot dusty hubbub of Ellsworth's main street.

CHAPTER THREE

Since they were both going to the hotel, Colbry untethered his horse and accompanied Mary Keyes in crossing
a chaotic cattle town street, which was always a case of risk-
ing life and limb. They didn't speak until they reached the
boardwalk of the Drover's Cottage, lined with about a dozen
men taking their ease in the chairs that lined the street side
of the hostelry, sitting in the shade and watching the dusty
pageantry of the foot, horseback and wagon traffic, seem-
ingly impervious to the heat and the choking dust. Before
they went inside Mary Keyes touched Colbry's arm, sidled
closer, took a look around and then up at him, shapely lips
slightly parted, giving her a breathless look.

"It's true, Luther and I discussed my trying to lure you
to a room in this hotel, and, well, while I was distracting
you, he would come in and knock you out and take your
money."

"He would have been disappointed, since I have about
three dollars to my name."

"Well, since he's locked up in jail, it would be all right
with me if you came up to my room." She gave him a look
that mixed desire with embarrassment. "I mean, if you
would like. And you could keep your money."

Colbry smiled faintly. He didn't try to pretend that he
wasn't interested. It had been a long push up from central

Texas and he was as virile as the next man and Mary Keyes was a very attractive woman. But he didn't trust her, didn't want to have to hurt her if she proved to be untrustworthy, and the fact that he had delayed meeting his new employer for too long nagged at him.

"I would be lying if I said I wasn't tempted, but I have to meet my boss." Colbry touched the brim of his disreputable hat. "Good luck to you, Miss Keyes. If you stick with your brother, you're going to need it." With that he turned and went inside the hotel.

He stopped dead in his tracks as soon as he crossed the threshold. The room he walked into was at least as big as a chapel and by frontier standards lavishly furnished, with ornately carved and plushly upholstered sofas and Victorian chairs along with marble-topped tables. Through a broad open doorway to one side he could see the restaurant with its rows of tables. There were two clerks at the long desk, and one of them informed him that there were a few available rooms. Aware of how Colbry had been gaping at his surroundings, the clerk informed him, with justifiable pride, that there were eighty-four rooms in all, the restaurant could seat a hundred guests, and he was welcome to stable his horse in the hotel's livery – all that before Colbry could tell him that he wasn't looking for lodging but rather sought a guest named Laurie Ruston. When the clerk gave him a long look-over, Colbry added that she was his boss. He was asked to wait in the lobby and was informed that a boy would be sent to inform Miss Ruston of his arrival. Colbry watched the boy head up the wide, carpeted staircase and took a seat in one of the chairs from whence, a few minutes later, he saw her come down those stairs, followed by the boy.

Laurie Ruston was a tall, slender woman in her twenties, with mahogany-brown hair done up in a long ponytail. She was dressed in a white blouse with the collar buttoned at the neck, a brown suede riding skirt, and black boots. Her descent down the stairs was both athletic and graceful, and when the boy pointed out Colbry, her stride was long and confident as she crossed the big room. As she drew closer Colbry decided that she was the most striking woman he had ever laid eyes on. He had known pretty women, most of them prostitutes, but their beauty had been painted on, and they looked considerably less attractive the next morning. Slender and taller than most females, Laurie Ruston's skin was tanned by constant outdoor life. Her brown eyes were big and bright. Her lips were full and finely sculpted. A warm and personable smile graced those lips and there was a friendly sparkle in those eyes. The hand she extended had a firm grip. Colbry's nostrils flared with the faint aroma of flowers that wafted his way as she came close and he remembered just in time to sweep the hat off his head.

"Mr. Colbry! I have very much looked forward to this moment. I am Laurie Ruston and I am very pleased to make your acquaintance."

Colbry wiped the palm of his right hand on the front of his shirt, which wasn't much cleaner than his hand, then took hers gently, shook it once, and quickly let go. "Miss Ruston. I just heard about your father from the sheriff. John Ruston was a good man."

Laurie's grateful smile faltered but she recovered quickly. "Thank you." She looked around and said, "Perhaps we can sit and talk?" She moved toward one of the settees and he followed, waiting until she had settled in one of them to sit in the nearest chair. He brushed the thick, unruly hair out of his eyes, feeling self-conscious, which was something new for him, and chastised himself for not taking a bath and washing off some of the caked-on sweat and dust that had collected ever since he had last bathed, if crossing the Red River with the Rocking Chair herd could be called that. There was a bathhouse in Ellsworth, a clapboard building off the main street where men could pay to wash themselves in large wooden barrels, but he didn't fancy bathing in water used by who knew how many men since morning.

"There's a cattle buyer here named Paxton," he told her. "Your father had sold to him in the past, so when I got to town I looked him up. He offers three dollars a head and will have the money in the morning. I hope that's okay with you. I was going to bring the herd up north and hold them near the railhead by nightfall."

Laurie nodded and smiled. "How many cattle?"

"Something more than nine hundred head, I'd say. We'll have the final count by suppertime."

She nodded, looking rather indifferent regarding the process of selling the Rocking Chair herd. Colbry noted that she was either a very good actress or the money didn't matter that much to her.

"What did you think of my father, Mr. Colbry? Please be honest."

Colbry nodded and looked around the room just to give himself a moment to consider his answer.

"Like I said, John Ruston was a good man, but a hard one. He had to be, to turn a handful of cows on a patch of land into one of the biggest and most profitable ranches in a state full of spreads. And he was tough enough to hold onto it. Rustling is big business these days. They sell the cattle they steal cheaper than the honest rancher, and some cattle buyers know who they are but buy what they offer anyway. More profit for them when they sell those beeves at the railhead. Your father was a man you never wanted to lie to or let down because if you did you'd be sorry. But he was a fair-minded man, too. Honest as the day is long. I was proud to ride for him."

She smiled pensively, and he caught a glimpse of soul-deep sorrow in her eyes. "I wish I had come back to see him," she sighed. "To be honest, I had a life of my own back East and I enjoyed it. The wonderful libraries, the amazing thoroughbred horses, the gorgeous clothes, the young men and the way they courted me. And the dances. So much dancing! It was all…very beguiling." Her shoulders rose and fell in a little shrug. "I used to write him letters when I was younger. But he wrote me back just one time. He wasn't much of a letter-writer, I suppose. As I grew older I got out of the habit. To be honest, sometimes I felt as though he just didn't want me around. I suspect he had other women in his life." She looked at Colbry with her brows lifted and it was clear she wanted him to speak to that suspicion.

Colbry shrugged. "I don't know, miss. I only worked for him a couple of years. All I can say is that while I knew him he never had anything to do with a woman." He shrugged, not wanting to say more, since he didn't know any more and wasn't going to speculate. The conversation had already moved too uncomfortably into the realm of the personal.

Laurie studied his expression for a moment, then nodded. "All right. Then do you know how…" She paused for a moment to handle her emotions, and it was clear by her stony expression and the glistening of her eyes. "Do you know how my father died?"

Colbry shook his head. "Afraid not. All I know is what was in the telegram sent up here to Sheriff Whitman." He paused, studying her closely. "Do you know?"

"No." Laurie looked down at her hands, which were clasped tightly. She softly cleared her throat and said, "Then maybe you would see fit to tell me about yourself?"

"I'm Texas-born. My father lived in Louisiana but went to Texas to help in its fight for independence from Mexico. He served with Colonel Fannin during the revolution against Santa Anna. Fannin's command was captured by the Mexicans and executed at Goliad by Santa Anna's command. Hundreds of men, including my father. My mother gave birth to me the day before. She died some years later, from pneumonia. Or maybe it was a broken heart." Morose memories led him astray for a moment, but he busted free of them, cleared his throat, and pressed on. "I got work as a wrangler on a few ranches. I was recruited into the Confederate Army when the war broke out. Wasn't happy about it. I was of the opinion that it was a mistake for Texas to join the Confederacy, and it was a bigger one to start a war against the Union. When all that was over I did some scouting for the army, then went back to working with horses when and where I could. That's what brought me to the Rocking Chair ranch. For some reason your father took a liking to me. Hired me as a wrangler. Before I knew it I was the one he trusted to get this herd to market."

Laurie nodded and smiled faintly as she tilted her head and murmured, "No family of your own?"

He shook his head. "Most of the good women who are worth hitching up with are already hitched. I don't reckon I'd be a very good catch, anyway."

"Or maybe you're underestimating yourself," she said.

The only women Colbry knew much about are soiled doves, but decided that was a topic he didn't care to discuss with his new boss. "I know a lot about horses and cattle but women, well, women are a mystery."

"We're supposed to be," she replied, then chuckled. "I am sure you must be very popular with the ladies," she said. She noticed how uncomfortable he seemed to be all of a sudden and abruptly changed the subject. "How many men with the herd?"

"Eleven, counting me and the cook, Alonso. A point man, four swing riders, two flankers, a couple of drag riders and a wrangler, which is me."

"Are they good at what they do?"

Colbry nodded. "They wouldn't be with the drive if they weren't. The drag riders are pretty green but hard workers and handy enough with the lariat."

"How many back at the ranch?"

"Another ten or so. Foreman's name is Trace Simmons. He knows his job, I guess. Never had much dealings with him, riding the line like I did."

"Oh? I thought you would be the foreman."

"No, ma'am. I just handled the drive. There's been some rustling and Trace said he needed to stay behind to deal with it. That suited me."

Laurie nodded and studied him for a moment, her head tilted slightly to one side, and Colbry knew she was sizing him up. "So you never wanted to be foreman? Since you're a trail boss, I thought for sure you aren't the type to shy away from responsibility."

"Trace has been with your father for a lot of years. He's a good foreman. Knows the trade as well as anyone. As for me, I'm content with what I do." Colbry pondered a moment in silence, then leaned forward, elbows planting on the table. "But I feel obliged to tell you this. I can't say that every man on the Rocking Chair payroll will take kindly to getting their orders from a woman."

Laurie smiled a wry smile. "Of course not. Do you feel the same way, Mr. Colbry?"

Colbry took a moment to answer, glancing through the nearest dust-grimed window at the cowtown street.

He rubbed his stubbled chin thoughtfully. He had never worked for a woman before and he did have to wonder if a young lady who had spent most of her life back East could run a ranch the size of the Rocking Chair, but he found himself liking Laurie Ruston. Why that was so, he had yet to figure out, since it went beyond attraction to a pretty, slender woman. His was a fairly jaundiced view of women, but then he hadn't known very many ladies. His experience was with saloon girls and brothel whores, the majority of whom were about as far from being a lady as you could get. He realized that he admired Laurie for being willing to step into the boots of a father who, for whatever reason, had sent her away. She was willing, but woefully ill-prepared, having been far removed from the open range for so long.

"I don't know," he heard himself say. "Tell you what. I'll ride with you to the Rocking Chair, and then I'll let you know if I'm staying. If you still want me to stay, that is."

She smiled warmly and nodded. "That's fair, though I don't know why I wouldn't want you to stay. We'll have time to get to know each other on the ride back. But there is one condition. You have to call me Laurie."

Colbry didn't return the smile. The thought of being so familiar with her made him uncomfortable. Or maybe it was because most cathouse jezebels offered their names right off. In fact, a few had given an entirely different name when he visited them at a later time. But he had just given her the assurance that he would continue to ride for the brand, at least for a little while longer, and he wasn't one to back away from what he considered a promise made.

"Whatever you say … Laurie. One more thing. A couple of years ago they laid down a railroad across the Territories, the Missouri, Kansas and Texas Railroad. Everybody calls it the Katy. You could get home faster if you took the train."

"Well, we could all go by rail, couldn't we."

"I reckon so. Most of the way, on a few different lines."

"But if I weren't here you and the men would ride back."

Colbry nodded. "Would cost a good amount of money to ship men and horses by rail."

Laurie mused for a handful of seconds, then shook her head. "I would rather ride back with you and the others. That way I can get to know you all better."

"The Territories are pretty dangerous, miss."

"Laurie."

"Pretty dangerous, Laurie."

"But I will have a dozen good men to protect me, won't I?"

"Well, we better find out how many are willing to stay with the brand," said Colbry.

Laurie nodded and smiled.

"I better get back to the herd and push your cattle up to the railhead so that the buyer can look them over and then pay you. And your cowhands are itching to come to town and cut loose. They won't be happy if they have to wait another night to do that."

"Just get word to me here at the hotel when you have the herd at the railhead. I would like to see it, and the rest of the crew."

"Come to think of it, might be a good idea if you were the one to pay them, too." He stood up and was about to turn to go when a thought struck him. "And you also need to find yourself a good horse."

She got to her feet when he did. "Oh I brought a horse with me. He's a fine specimen indeed, Mr. Colbry."

"You shipped a horse all that way?"

"He isn't just a horse." She fairly glowed with pride. "Beholden is a Kentucky thoroughbred. I've raised him from a foal." She extended a hand.

"Well, not sure I've ever seen a bluegrass thoroughbred in Texas," remarked Colbry.

"You're about to." Laurie stood up, and surprised him again by extending a hand. He took it and she gripped his hand firmly and gave it two shakes. "I'm counting on you, Mr. Colbry. Please don't let me down."

He assured her that he wouldn't and lingered in the hotel lobby, watching her go back up the stairs. Near the top of the staircase she looked over her shoulder, smiling still, and waved at him.

Turning to leave the Drover's Cottage, he wondered what the hell he had gotten himself into.

A couple of hours later he rode into the camp set out by a creek that meandered through the wide open prairie, and where the Rocking Chair herd was being held. The sun was a blazing orange orb in the western sky, no more than a couple of hours shy of setting. There were a half-dozen cowboys in camp, most of them collected around the chuckwagon. The cook, Alonso, had built a fire and made some coffee. Four more were watching over the herd held a bit west of camp.

Alonso was an elderly Mexican. No one knew exactly how old he was. In fact, some speculated that even Alonso didn't know for sure. But he was hands down the best hash slinger Colbry had ever met, and that included quite a few able hash-slingers in various gold camps and military bivouacs. Alonso had never told anyone about his past, not even John Ruston, but some of the Rocking Chair hands agreed that if he had ever had a family he didn't have one any longer. In fact, he acted like the cowboys were his sons. He was without question dedicated to their good health. He was also adept at using herbs to cure what ailed them, even a paste that could drain some of the poison out of a diamondback rattler's bite, giving the victim at least a small chance of surviving. When Colbry showed up, Alonso was berating the cowboys to eat a good meal before they hit town and filled up on beer and rotgut whiskey.

The cowboys' mounts were tethered to a rope tied to the chuckwagon on one end and an old cottonwood on the creek bank at the other. The mules that pulled the wagon had been tied to another line after being taken down to the creek to drink. Alonso had sourdough biscuits browning on big blackened iron pans set on the rocks rimming the hot coals. Beans, which the cowboys called "Pecos strawberries," were simmering in a Dutch oven, a cast iron pot with legs placed over the coals. Colbry could smell the beans and coffee from afar, and his stomach grumbled to remind him that he hadn't eaten since daybreak, a breakfast consisting of hard tack and creek water. After that, he would head back to Ellsworth.

As he dismounted and wrapped the reins around the tether rope for the horses, a lanky, square-jawed cowboy named Burr Welken left the company of the other cowboys, who had gathered near the wagon, paused at the camp fire to pour coffee into a tin cup and brought it over. Colbry sipped the coffee, finding it, as usual, strong and bitter, then said "Thanks, Burr."

"So how's Ellsworth?" asked the other.

"Hot. Dirty. Busy."

"And the women? Hot, dirty and busy too?"

"I expect so." Colbry thought about Mary Keyes. "Most of them, anyway."

Burr grinned. "Just the way I like 'em." Burr Welken was an old hand, broad and solid, his face creased and dark as black walnut. He had worked for the Rocking Chair brand for more than a decade and was as honest, dependable and hard-working as any man Colbry had ever met.

Alonso came up with a plate of beans topped with a piece of bread and offered it to Colbry with a single word. "Eat!"

Colbry looked at the plate, and though he would have vouched for Alonso as one of the best trail cooks he had ever met, he discovered that he didn't have much of an appetite. Nonetheless, he took the plate and said "Gracias" and Alonso went away happy, since the old Mexican took it personally when his grub was refused or not consumed.

"How much is the old man likely to make from those ornery bags of bones?" asked Burr. He gestured in the general direction of the grazing herd.

"A fair price. But Ruston won't see it."

Burr's bushy brows furrowed. "What do you mean by that?"

Colbry handed over the telegram Sheriff Whitman had given him and watched the top hand read it. Burr was a hard man, but the news the telegram conveyed hit him hard, literally rocking him back on his heels. When he handed it back to Colbry, his hand was shaking a little.

Welken swallowed the lump in his throat. "Best man I ever knew," he said, sorrowfully.

Some of the other trail hands by the wagon had been watching and noticed Burr's reaction. One of them, Emil Canfield, a tall lanky young man with unruly yellow hair that looked like straw sticking out from under his hat, walked over. Colbry could tell by Emil's furrowed brow that, while he couldn't have overheard, he sensed that something was wrong but he wasn't going to ask straight out.

"So, is Ellsworth ready for us, boss?" he asked Colbry.

Colbry smiled. "Ready to take all your wages, anyway." It was a humorous warning but also a sincere one.

"And your virginity," said Burr, and smiled faintly at the embarrassed expression on the other's face.

Colbry handed the plate of untouched food to Burr and then walked past the young cowpoke, moving closer to the other men nearer the chuck wagon, the telegram still in hand. "Gather around and listen tight, boys. I've got some sad news. John Ruston is dead."

The cowboys looked at one another with expressions of shock and disbelief, quickly replaced by varying degrees of sadness or disappointment based on how long they had ridden for the brand or how much they had liked their boss.

"We still get paid, right?" asked one, a fellow by the name of Red Russell.

"How did he die?" asked another.

"What happens to the ranch?" queried a third.

"You will all get paid tonight after we move the cows to the railhead and they get counted. I don't know how Mr. Ruston died. The telegram didn't say. As for the Rocking Chair, Mr. Ruston's daughter has been waiting for us in Ellsworth. She is going to keep the ranch, so you all still have a job if you want one."

He looked at each of them in turn, trying to read their reactions.

"I don't know," said one, shrugging his shoulders.

"Never worked for a woman before," said another, and he clearly wasn't enthused. "You gonna still ride for the brand, Cord?"

Colbry nodded. "A while, anyway. I told her I would."

"You think she can handle it?" asked Russell..

"Time will tell. But I know one thing. John Ruston would want us to stick by his daughter." Colbry knew that this would matter to at least some of the hands. There were some nods, shrugs, morose head shakes and subdued murmuring among the men, and he added, "You boys think it over and let me know when you get paid. Grab some grub if you need it, then Emil, you and Hardy and Emmett go watch the herd and send the others in to eat. What time is it, Burr?"

The burly top hand fished a stemwinder, out of his canvas pants. "Quarter after three."

"We move the herd in thirty minutes."

"I have an idea," said another man, whose name was Tom Selman. He was a big man without an ounce of fat on him, and dull brown eyes that would fasten on a person in a cold and impersonal way. Colbry didn't particularly like him but couldn't say why, since he did his share of the work and did it adequately.

"I say we split the money between ourselves and forget about Ruston's daughter," said Selmon. "If we get three dollars a head we'll all make about two hundred dollars, more than twice what we'll get paid in wages for three months of pushing that herd all the way up here." He looked around at the other cowboys, trying to gauge their reaction to his proposal. "She don't need it. She'll still have the spread." His gaze fastened suspiciously on Colbry. "Think about it, Cord, before you say no. We don't owe her nothing."

Colbry's expression had hardened during Selman's pitch. Then he grimly shook his head. "That's not going to happen. I'm not a cattle rustler and you're not going to steal the whole damn herd while I'm above snakes."

Selman looked at him, sullen. Colbry's gaze was as cold as it had been in the Ellsworth alley earlier that day. Watching the other man's eyes, he could peripherally see Selman's gun hand, and if the cowboy had pulled his iron, Colbry was ready to plug him at point blank range. Selman must have realized this, because he shrugged and took a step back, still scowling, but with his hand well away from his holstered pistol.

Chapter Four

Colbry got back to Ellsworth at sunset, this time from the north, crossing the railroad tracks to ride into town. The hitching posts were lined with horses shoulder to shoulder, since there were at least a hundred cowboys from ten different herds rewarding themselves for two or three months pushing ornery cows north to the railhead by spending their hard-earned wages on whiskey and loose women. Soon enough, mused Colbry, Rocking Chair riders would be joining them.

He found a spot to hitch Boots, then walked down to the Drovers Cottage and went inside to tell the man behind the counter in the lobby that he was there to see Laurie Ruston. The clerk asked him his name and, when Colbry gave it, told him that the lady had just left and he assumed that Ranson's Livery had been her destination because she often went there. He provided directions.

The livery was at the eastern end of one of the town's cross streets, and when Colbry arrived with Boots in tow a man came up to him, eyeing the tall, lanky buckskin, and began to regale Colbry with details of the fine horses he had on hand, all of them for sale at a reasonable price. Or trade, he added, looking at Boots again. Colbry shook his head and told him why he was visiting as he dismounted and tied his horse to the top rail of the corral that fronted the livery's barn-like structure.

Laurie was inside, grooming Beholden, her tall, handsome, pitch black thoroughbred. One look at her horse and he could tell Beholden was more horse than the vast majority he had seen or ridden out on the frontier. Laurie was dressed just as she had been at their first meeting, and smiled warmly when she saw him and stepped out of the stall that housed the horse. He told her that the herd was near the railhead and he was on his way to see the cattle buyer and wondered if she wanted to come along.

Laurie replied that she was hungry and would like to have supper before riding out to see the herd. Colbry didn't get the sense that she was at all apprehensive about meeting the crew. He left his horse at the livery, paid the owner a modest amount to keep an eye on Boots, and when Laurie was done grooming Beholden they walked over to the Drovers Cottage. They both ordered steaks. Laurie asked him what he knew about her family's past. He told her that John Ruston had not been one to talk about his past, and that included his family.

"I am," she said. "My grandmother and grandfather were born and married in Mississippi. He was in the river trade. His first wife was the daughter of a wealthy New Orleans merchant. She died quite young of cholera. His second wife was the daughter of a woman who worked for father as a cook and housekeeper. She died of snakebite. My mother was the widow of a United States Army officer who died at Veracruz during the War of Mexico. A few years after my birth she was carried away by the outlaws that prowled the Natchez Trace. She hid me in the well bucket, lowered halfway down. I still remember her screams. I started crying.

Later I thought that maybe she was screaming to drown out the sounds I was making.

"I was rescued by cavalrymen who were trying to catch up with those outlaws." She paused, toying with her food. She had eaten less than half of the steak and Colbry wondered if she had lost her appetite. "My father searched for her for almost a year. I think all of what I just told you had to do with his decision to send me East. That and to get a proper education. I was fortunate to gain entry to Vasser, an all-female college. The first of its kind in the country, I believe. I think my father thought our family was cursed, since so many had died badly, and he didn't want me growing up in the South anyway. He thought that there was going to be a war, and if so the South would lose and suffer the consequence." Glancing up at him with a pensive smile and added, "You never thought about having a family of your own?" she asked.

Colbry didn't much care for talking about his past but Laurie had not only shared a great deal of information with him but she was his boss now, and deserved to know about his past. He considered his answer while chewing on some steak.

"I did a lot of wandering. Passed on an opportunity or two that now I realize maybe I should have taken.. Always wanted to see what's on the other side of the next hill, you know. I reckon a person only gets so many chances."

"You might not be out of chances. One never knows," she murmured, then pushed the plate away, her steak half-eaten, and laid a hand over her belly. "I've had my fill and then some. But, please, take your time."

Colbry took another bite and then tossed his napkin on the table. "I'm done, too. Ready to see your herd?"

Laurie said she was. He remembered his manners and held her chair while she rose. He dug into a pocket, hoping he had enough money to pay the bill but she stopped him. "You work for me now, remember?" she said, smiling.

She paid and they left The Drover's Cottage, collected their mounts at Ransom's and rode north to the railhead.

While she saddled Beholden he admitted that he had cut a deal with a buyer the day before.

"I'm thinking now I crossed the line when I did," he confessed. "They were your cattle and you had the right to make the deal."

Laurie just shook her head, smiling warmly. "You know much more about all that than I do. Besides, I'm not all that interested in cattle."

That startled him. "What do you mean? If you're not interested in the cattle trade, why did you come back?"

"Because it's my birthplace. And my birthright. I have always thought of it as home. But I am not about cattle. I want to raise horses."

Colbry nodded, as though he completely understood, even though he didn't.

The dismounted at the station. The train that had been on the tracks when Colbry had returned to town from the north was gone now. They ran day and night this time of year, carrying cattle and passengers eastward. So from the station platform Colbry had an unobstructed view northward. There were two herds out on the plains, partially obscured by hovering clouds of dust, but his eyes were keen and he could identify the mounts of some of the cowpunchers keeping the Rocking Chair herd under control. He glanced at Laurie and pointed. "Those are your cattle. We'll know the count as soon as we make sure about the deal I struck with that buyer I told you about."

They walked inside the station. Paxton was there, talking to three men whom Colbry guessed were also cattle buyers. When Paxton recognized Colbry he broke away from the other men and came forward, gazing curiously at Laurie. He extended a hand, smiling pleasantly.

"You must be John Ruston's daughter. I am very pleased to make your acquaintance. I am Orville Paxton, out of St. Louis, and I struck a deal for your herd with this fellow…" he nodded in Colbry's direction "…earlier today. Are you satisfied with that deal, miss?"

Laurie took the proffered hand and shook it, nodding. "Indeed I am."

Colbry turned to Laurie and said, "Why don't you stay here. I'll see to getting your cattle over to the pens so they can be counted."

It took over an hour to bring the herd up and run them through the pen chutes for a count, with both Colbry and Burr Welken making the count and Laurie looking on for a while before returning to the station. When the count was done, Colbry also went back inside the station, covered in a fresh coat of dust from head to toe. Laurie was sitting at a small table by the windows with Paxton. They were drinking coffee provided by the station master, who was making some money on the side by keeping the buyers that frequented the place plied with coffee, beer and whiskey.

"Nine hundred and thirty eight head of prime beef, by my count," Colbry told them.

"Two thousand eight hundred and fourteen dollars," said Paxton almost immediately. A few moments later, the bill of sale was signed. He drank the rest of his coffee and smiled across at Laurie. "Whenever you're ready, miss, we can head on down to the bank and I will get you your money."

Laurie said she was ready. While she walked with Paxton, Colbry rode Boots, bringing her thoroughbred along with him. He went inside the bank with them and stood back to watch Paxton retrieve some of his funds from a clerk and then count out the payment with Laurie. She had the good sense to turn to Colbry and hand him the thick bundle of paper currency.

"Since you have the gun, perhaps you would look after this for me?"

Colbry shoved the bundle into a pocket of his canvas pants and Paxton nodded his approval of her decision.

"There are probably a few eagle-eyed bad characters who will figure out you've had a big payday. I am fairly well known as a buyer. But this fellow looks like he can handle trouble." He extended a hand to Colbry, who shook it. Then Paxton touched the brim of his hat to Laurie with a big smile. "I look forward to doing more business with you in the future, Miss Ruston." Then he took his leave.

When they were outside the station, Laurie asked Colbry how much of a profit Paxton would make when he sold the Rocking Chair herd.

"I don't know for sure and right now Paxton doesn't either," he replied, securing the money in his saddlebag. "Depends on the market, I reckon. Every year more and more cattle are shipped east. My guess would be maybe twenty-five, thirty dollars a head. But he has a lot of expenses, too. The cost of shipping the herd and then hiring men to hold and handle it until it's sold. No idea how much that adds up to, but it's bound to be a bundle of money."

Watching him put the proceeds of the cattle sale into his saddlebags, Laurie asked, "Should we take that to a bank?"

Colbry thought about it a moment, then shrugged. "That's up to you."

She put her hands on her hips and tilted her head, smiling. "No. I want you to tell me what you think!"

Colbry looked around, making sure no one was passing close enough to overhear.

"I would carry it with us. We should have most of the hands traveling back with us and if we stay off the main trails we'll probably be okay. And I wouldn't trust banks with this kind of money. Especially not a bank down in Texas."

She nodded. "I just wondered. I mean we have to pass through the Indian Territory. I've heard some stories about that place. What did my father do?"

"He took the cash home himself. It's not Indians that you have to worry about until we get close to the Rocking Chair. There are some outlaw gangs in the Territory but, again, we won't be alone." He looked at her, his brows knit. "You tell me. It's your call, Miss Ruston."

Laurie thought about it a moment, then made up her mind and smiled at him.

"I trust your judgment. We take it with us. And don't call me Miss Ruston again." She wagged a finger at him, but now her smile was broader and brighter.

Colbry walked Boots back up the street toward the rail-head, and this time Laurie walked beside him. It was time to pay the Rocking Chair cowboys. Now and then her shoulder brushed his and when he glanced at her she had a smile waiting for him.

At the station he explained that he would tell her how much she owed each cowboy, then left her in the company of Paxton and rode out to the herd. He rounded up all but four riders, who would assist the buyer in loading the cattle into rail cars, roughly fifty head fitting in each car. The process took the rest of the day and it was about sundown when he went inside the station to fetch Laurie after telling the Rocking Chair hands to wait on the platform. He handed her the cash he had kept for safe-keeping.

Taking her out to meet the Rocking Chair crew, he watched the faces of the cowboys as they got their first look at John Ruston's daughter. None of them could take their eyes off her – until she looked directly at one, who then averted his eyes. It wasn't just because she had their hard-earned wages but also because they hadn't seen a woman in months, and possibly had never seen one who was so comely.

"I'll call you up by name," Colbry informed the hands, "and Miss Ruston here will pay you what you're owed. Then the first four paid will need to ride back to the herd and replace the men out there so they can come in. Andy, you're first."

A rawboned young man came up, his spurs ringing on the scarred wooden planks of the platform and grabbed his hat off his head as he stood in front of Laurie, staring at her open-mouthed as Colbry told her how much to pay him. Apparently he wasn't thinking about money because when she offered him the bills he belatedly looked down at them and said "Oh! Thank you, ma'am." and performed a stiff, awkward little bow that made some of his fellow riders laugh. One of them said, "You sure are a lady's man, Andy!"

Colbry called up three more, then fastened his gaze on Tom Selman and called him up. When Laurie paid him he counted the bills twice, then looked up at Colbry.

"Should be more," he muttered.

Colbry knew what he meant and gestured at him to get back. "That's what you earned and what you're owed. And by the way, you're fired."

Sullen, Selman looked up sharply, and his surprise quickly turned into belligerence. "You can't fire me. She owns the ranch." He pointed at Laurie with his chin.

"Yes, he can," said Laurie. "I don't know you. Any of you. I trust his judgment."

Selman glared at her, silent for a moment, fist clenched round the bills with which he had been paid. Colbry spoke up to capture his attention.

"He wanted us to take the full price for the herd and split it up," he told Laurie. "He can't be trusted."

She was startled. Then her brows knit as she fastened a cold stare on Selman. "You no longer ride for my brand, Mr. Selman."

Selman's dark, angry gaze fixed on Colbry. "You son-of-a-bitch," he muttered, and then threw a wild punch with the hand that was full of paper money.

Colbry wasn't surprised. Selman was a prideful bully and he had just been humiliated in front of his compadres. Stepping into the punch, Colbry blocked the swing with his left arm and hammered a right into the other man's body, just below the sternum. Selman doubled over with the wind knocked out of him. But he put his head down and rammed into Colbry. Their legs entangled and they fell, Colbry landing hard with the bigger man on top of him. Though this knocked the wind out of him, he managed to leverage Selman to the side by throwing his right leg over the other man and rolling him onto his back. Straddling Selman, he bounced the man's skull off the weathered boards of the platform with a short, powerful punch. Colbry was quick and limber, but his opponent was strong as a bull. Selman growled and bucked him off. Sprawling to the side, Colbry tried to get to his feet first but Selman was faster and threw a powerhouse right hook that knocked him down again. Colbry's skull bounced off the platform and his vision briefly darkened as he nearly blacked out. His blurred vision cleared just enough for him to catch a glimpse of the other man leering down at him, raising a leg to stomp on his rib cage.

Rolling onto his left side, Colbry swung his right leg into the leg that Selman was, for an instant, balanced on, and his adversary went down like a cut tree. The impact of his body made a tremor ripple through the planking. Colbry rolled over and pushed himself to his feet in time to launch a kick at Selman's head as the latter started to get up. But Selman caught his leg and pushed it to one side and again Colbry went down. Selman growled a curse as he got to his feet and saw his opponent roll over and push to his feet again. When the surly cowhand lowered his head and shoulders and charged like a bull, Colbry smashed an uppercut into the man's face as he quickly sidestepped out of Selman's path. With a grunt of pain, the other man went down. He tried to push up again but Colbry bent over and punched him in the back of the head and Selman's face bounced off the platform. His body went limp.

Wheezing and dizzy, Colbry staggered then found his balance and took a step away from the other man with his fists up and ready to continue the fight. But Selman, sprawled face down on the platform, didn't get up. He didn't move. Colbry nudged him with the toe of a boot but Selman didn't respond. Colbry relaxed and straightened up, wiping blood out of his eye.

Laurie was moving closer to him, clearly concerned for his well-being, but Colbry threw out an arm to hold her at bay and took two steps closer to the other cowboys who had been watching the fight. Some of them were apprehensive, others watched him grimly.

"Are any more of you unhappy with your pay?" snarled Colbry. His blood was hot and he was more than ready to fight someone else, despite the fact that he wasn't in any condition to.

Some of them exchanged glances, and then most of them shook their heads. The others just watched him warily.

Nodding, Colbry glanced around at Laurie, then, turning back to the men, called out four more names.

When all the cowboys had been paid, Laurie came up to Colbry with a lace-edged handkerchief in her hand and reached up to dab blood off his face, even though he insisted he was okay. It was a lie. He was dizzy still, and couldn't seem to keep from swaying in place.

"No you aren't," she said. "I saw a doctor's office down the street. We're going down there right now." She saw him open his mouth and knew he was of a mind to protest and added, "No! You're coming with me and don't argue."

She wrapped her arm around his and pulled him close and they walked side by side off the platform. They paused long enough for her to collect the reins of Boots and Beholden and then headed into town.

Chapter Five

Laid out on a table with his shirt open in the back room of a two-room clapboard building along Ellsworth's main street, Colbry felt dizzy and nauseous as a doctor loomed over him, a tall, thin elderly man named Ruhle who was poking and prodding his upper torso, which was already bruised, none too gently. The room was small, with barely enough room for the operating table, a glass-front Victorian cabinet containing medical supplies, and a shelf with a small water barrel on it alongside a tin sink built into it. Laurie stood on the other side of the table, looking worried.

"Anything broken, doctor?" she asked, impatiently.

"Ribs seem intact," replied the doctor. He clutched Colbry's jaw and turned his patient's head to the left and right, then added, "Spinal cord is okay, too." He studied his patient's face for a moment, his head tilted slightly. "But your face looks like you got trampled by a herd of wild horses, cowboy."

"Feels like it, too," said Colbry. It was a mumbled reply because his jaw ached and his lips were swollen and it hurt to form words. He had a raging headache and his body was so sore that even getting on the examination table had been a real chore. Blood was running into his right eye so he kept it closed.

"You have a gash about two inches long above your eye," said the sawbones. "It's going to need stitches. And you may have a mild concussion. Now I don't have any morphine. That's mighty hard to come by out here. But opium isn't, if you want it, because sewing you up will hurt like the dickens."

Colbry shook his head. "No. No opium." Most towns of good size had opium dens and some chuckwagons were known to carry a supply. But he had seen the effects of opium on a few of the soiled doves he had met, and had heard of many more who had died of their addiction. "But I'll take a swig of the whiskey I smell on your breath."

The physician was taken aback. He threw an embarrassed glance at Laurie and started to protest his innocence. "I don't know…" and then paused, thought better of it and finished with "…if that's a good idea but, very well. Whiskey can thin your blood but I suppose a sip or two will be okay." He left the table and went to his desk, returned with a bottle of Old Judge, uncorked it with his teeth, and poured a little into a shot glass.

Colbry raised his head and the doctor put the glass to his lips. He drank every drop, put his head down and gasped. "Let's get to it."

The doctor loomed over him, a cloth that was damp with camphor in one hand, a threaded needle in the other. Colbry glanced at Laurie, who wasn't looking the least bit squeamish. She gave him a reassuring smile and grabbed his right hand. He tensed as the wound was cleaned with the camphor, and winced as the needle punctured his skin, and he felt every millimeter of the catgut thread that ran through the holes the needle made. He felt blood trickling down into his hair on the side of his head. The wound took eight stitches and Colbry breathed an audible sigh of relief when the task was done. The doctor lightly pressed the cloth against the wound for a minute, checked the bleeding, applied pressure with the cloth again, and then nodded, satisfied with his work and his patient.

"Not the first time you've been stitched up, I'm thinking," he said, as he discarded the bloody cloth in a tin bucket and got a new one to dab at the blood and minor cuts, of which there were several, on his patient's face.

"No," said Colbry hoarsely, remembering the day he had dug an Apache bullet out of his side and then stitched up the bullet hole himself. At the time he had carried a flask of whiskey, and he had taken a swallow of its contents and then used the rest of the whiskey to cauterize the wound. It was a day of pure agony he would not forget.

The sawbones rinsed his hand in the water bucket, helped his patient sit up and then applied a tight dressing round Colbry's head. "If you don't mind me saying so, I would guess that you were in a fist fight. But a bare fist didn't split your head open like this."

"I got knocked down some. Reckon it might have been a nail in the flooring of the train platform."

The doctor nodded, smiling faintly. "Did you happen to win this fight?"

"Well, I was the one that walked away." He glanced at Laurie. "With a little help."

A few minutes later the doctor had done all he could do apart from offering Colbry an opium solution for the pain, which was declined. Ruhle gave Laurie a roll of clean bandages and a small bottle of camphor. With help, Colbry got off the table and Laurie paid his bill, then held onto his arm as they walked out onto the boardwalk. Colbry had a splitting headache and a slight limp as she steered him down the street to the Drover's Cottage. When they were in the lobby at the foot of the staircase up to the rooms he stopped and threw a look around. The clerk at the counter and a couple of other spectators were looking at him and Laurie.

"Where are we going?" he asked.

"To my room. You need to lay down before you fall down, and you really must get some rest."

Colbry balked as she tried to proceed and she turned and looked at him sternly, shaking her head. "I don't care what people might say. If you insist, I will see if there is a spare room, but I doubt that there is." She tugged gently on his arm and he gave in and let her help him up the stairs.

Once inside the room she helped him lay down on the bed and pulled off his boots, poured a little water from the pitcher on the bureau into a glass and held his head up while he sipped from the glass. The room was darkening as the sun was setting, so she lit the kerosene lamp on the bureau. Then she sat down in a high-backed chair beside the room's single window, which was open, and sighed wearily.

"How many of the ranch hands do you think will quit?" she asked.

"Don't know," he said. "Most will spend a couple of days here, spend their pay and then, when they're broke, decide if they're heading back to the Rocking Chair or wander off to find work with some other spread. Most of the cowboys who stayed behind have been working there for at least a year or two. A few of the ones who brought the herd up haven't been. I can vouch for a couple, like Burr Welken and Emil Canfield. Then there's Alonso, the cook. He's been around a lot longer than I have."

"And you will stay, I hope," she said, with a smile. "My father entrusted the herd to you, so you must be trustworthy. Did he make you the foreman?"

"No. The foreman is Trace Simmons. He stayed behind as there's been a rustling problem."

"What kind of man is he?"

Colbry shrugged. He didn't particularly like Simmons, which was one reason he had gladly taken the line rider job, a job most cowboys tried to avoid, since it involved months of being alone and too far from town to blow off steam in some cantina. Simmons knew cowboying, but he had let being ranch foreman go to his head, and he expected the Rocking Chair cowboys to kowtow to him. "He knows his trade," was all Colbry said, which was true enough.

Laurie was thoughtfully quiet for a few minutes, then said, "I would like to leave as soon as possible. I want to see my birthplace again. Will you be able to ride in a couple of days?"

Colbry turned his head to look at her. "I can ride now. But we should go back with Burr and the others who aim to stay on with the Rocking Chair. There are renegades in the Indian Territory, and bandits along the Red River. I still think taking the MKT Railroad would be safer, But then again, it's been held up by robbers pretty regular."

Laurie nodded, then stood up, checked the dressing on his head, and said, "I'm starving. I will go check on Beholden and put your horse up at the livery, then I'll have some supper. I'll bring you a plate. You get some rest, and if you are asleep when I get back you'll have steak and potatoes for breakfast."

"Thank you, miss."

She was turning for the door, but glanced back to him and said, "I told you. Call me Laurie." She said it sternly, but her smile reached her green eyes.

Colbry passed out as soon as she closed the door behind her.

He woke with morning sunlight pouring through the window. Laurie was sleeping soundly in the chair. She had pulled off her boots and he could see one of her legs below the knee and her bare feet. The top two buttons of the white blouse she wore were unbuttoned. For a moment he gazed at her, wondering if she had the grit it would take to run the Rocking Chair ranch, and wondering, too, if he would be doing her a favor if he could talk her into returning to her life back East. But there wasn't much chance of that. He realized that if she was half as stubborn as her father he wouldn't be able to.

A rapping on the door woke her. She glanced at Colbry, who was grimacing as he tried to prop himself up on an elbow and reach his pistol, the gun belt draped over one of the headboard's posts. She gestured for him to stay down, went to the door and called through it.

"Who is it?"

"Sheriff Whitman."

She unlatched and opened the door, stepping to one side to let the lawman into the room. Whitman gave her a nod while he swept the hat off his head.

"Morning, ma'am. Came to see how Cordell is doing." He stepped to the foot of the bed and frowned as he studied Colbry's face. Laurie shut the door, then turned and leaned against it. "Well you look like warmed-over hell," Whitman told Colbry affably. "One of the Rocking Chair cowboys tells me it was a man named Tom Selman that did that to you."

"That's right."

"Selman got the worst of it," said Laurie.

"Well I can't seem to find that man," remarked the Ellsworth sheriff. "We have three doctors here and none of them have treated a cowboy for anything more than ptomaine or a hangover. So maybe he rode out, Or maybe he crawled into a hole." He turned to Laurie." To be on the safe side I will leave a deputy outside your door." He glanced back at Colbry and held up a hand. "Don't tell me you can handle him. I just don't want anybody shot dead, or any harm to come to this young lady." He looked back at Laurie. "Are you riding back to Texas with your cowhands. ma'am?"

"Whenever Mr. Colbry can ride."

Colbry grimaced. He didn't fancy being coddled. "I can ride," he grumbled.

"Maybe you shouldn't if the doctor is right and you have a concussion," said Laurie.

"I've been hurt worse than this and stayed in the saddle," he grumbled.

Whitman chuckled. "You got your hands full with this one," he told Laurie as he turned for the door. Then he snapped his fingers and turned back to look at Colbry. "By the way, since you weren't going to stick around for a trial, I had to let Luther Keyes out of jail. I advised him and his sister to get out of town. If they don't there ain't much I can do. So watch your back, cowboy. Keyes doesn't strike me as a man who forgets and forgives." Whitman touched his hat brim as he gave Laurie a nod. "Good luck, miss."

Laurie smiled at Whitman and nodded. "I can handle this cowboy."

"I don't doubt it, miss"

As Whitman left the room, Colbry caught a glimpse of a lean, tow-headed man with a badge and a star standing in the hallway, the sheriff's deputy.

Closing the door, Laurie moved to the bed and took a closer look at the dressing round Colbry's skull. "Looks like the doctor did a good job sewing you up. I'll change the bandages as soon as I get back."

"Where are you going?"

She had moved to the dresser, which, with the bed and the chair she had slept in were all the furnishings that would fit in the room. She washed her face with the water in a large ceramic bowl, then picked up a hand mirror and began brushing her long brown hair. "Going to check on our horses and then grab some breakfast. I will bring you a plate."

Colbry slowly lowered his head onto the pillow. "Take the deputy with you."

Laurie looked over her shoulder at him as she buttoned the collar of her blouse and then sat down in the chair to pull on her riding boots. "Absolutely not. Get some rest. I'll be back soon. Then you can tell me about this man, Luther Keyes." She tilted her head slightly and looked at him a moment, long enough to make Colbry wonder what was on her mind. Then she told him.

"I've known you for less than a day but I already know one thing about you, Mr. Colbry. You have a real talent for getting into trouble."

And with that she smiled warmly, grabbed the door key and went out, locking the door behind her.

At dawn the next day, Colbry had decided he couldn't abide being in bed one more minute. Laurie was sleeping soundly in the chair and despite a throbbing headache he managed to rise and get his boots on and the gun-rig buckled around his waist without making much more noise than an Apache would have made. But she hadn't left the key in the lock and it wasn't on the dresser so he had to settle for standing at the window, holding the thin curtain aside to study the street and watch Ellsworth wake up. Having hunted Apaches and living to tell the tale, he had an iron grip on impatience and didn't usually let it get the best of him.

He was still there twenty minutes later when Laurie stirred, stretched and yawned. Her eyes widened when she saw Colbry standing there, jumped out of the chair and took two steps to reach him, firmly gripping his arm, a concerned expression on her face.

"What are you doing up?" she asked. "You shouldn't be on your feet until the doctor sees you again."

"Most of the hands are probably low on funds after a night on the town.. We need to find Alonso. Any of your hands who plan to go back to the Rocking Chair will rendezvous with him today and escort the wagon back. They might even be aiming to head out today."

"Where will we find him?"

"He'll be at the last camp we made, north of the railhead."

She nodded, sat back down and quickly pulled her boots on. In moments she was ready to go. He insisted on handling her single bag and they went down to the lobby of the Drovers Cottage where she paid her bill. Then it was on to the livery, where they saddled their horses and Laurie paid the livery owner. Then they rode out of Ellsworth, heading north, Laurie's single bag secured to her saddle. Colbry was edgy until they crossed the tracks and rode out into the wide-open plains, checking every man on the street and every alleyway for Selman or another Rocking Chair hand, not to mention Luther Keyes and his sister.

It was a warm day and the sun was ablaze in a cloudless, bright-blue sky. The pens around the railhead were, of course, packed with cattle, a cloud of dust hovering low over them. He and Laurie swung wide around another herd being moved toward the pens. It took them more than a half hour to reach the Rocking Chair camp. Since there was only the horse remuda to herd, most of the cowboys were lounging around the chuckwagon. Colbry did a head count. The old Mexican pot-rustler, Alonso, was as usual cooking up some beef steaks for lunch and of course there was Arbuckle coffee. Hot "brown gargle" was always available. Burr Welken and Emil Canfield were present, and three other hands. With the pair watching over the horses, that made seven hands. Selman and three other cowboys were gone.

When Colbry and Laurie dismounted, Burr came up to take charge of their horses and Alonso came over with two cups of coffee. Colbry felt obliged to accept, and Laurie did likewise. He watched her, curious, as she sipped the steaming hot brew and smiled at her expression after she did.

"It's strong enough to float a horseshoe," he remarked.

She thanked Alonso in Spanish, which pleased the cook immensely. By then Burr and the other cowboys had gathered around. They were curious about Laurie, and the condition of Colbry's face.

"Bill Selman came through a bit after dawn this morning," drawled Burr. "Said you and he had a quarrel and that he got the better of you." He clapped a big hand on Colbry's shoulder. "But having seen his face and yours, I'd say you came out in better shape than he did." He turned to Laurie with a big smile and touched the brim of his hat. "Nice to meet ya, miss. Name is Burr Welken." Then he half-turned and pointed out the other Rocking Hand cowboys, naming them. They all said their howdies, most with hat in hand. Some were too shy to gape at her, but a couple did just that. To her credit, she was all smiles and shook hands with each and every one of them, repeating their names as she committed them to memory. When she was done, Colbry stepped in and spoke to all the hands.

"So, since you are still here I reckon that means you're willing to ride for Miss Ruston, which is what Big John would expect of you," he said, resorting to the name by which most of the Rocking Chair hands referred to their now-dead boss. "Is that so?"

They all either nodded or affirmed it vocally.

"Then after you eat we'll head out."

Laurie smiled the warmest, happiest smile that Colbry had ever seen.

"Good," she murmured. "I can't wait to get home."

As they were riding south out of Ellsworth, Colbry spotted Mary Keyes standing outside of a saloon called the Holy Moses. She was conversing with a cowboy leaning against the wall, and seemed to be flirting. There was a carpetbag at her feet. He smiled faintly as he and Laurie rode on, assuming Luther was in the saloon and probably up to no good, and the carpetbag reminded him that Chancey Whitman had told the Keyes to leave town.

He had stopped looking by the time Luther Keyes came barging through the watering hole's batwing door to grab his sister's arm and pull her away from the cowboy and march her down the boardwalk to the alley two doors further down. In the alley were a pair of horses, tethered to an old buckboard. Keyes paused at the corner of the building to watch the Rocking Chair crew leaving Ellsworth, then turned to his sister. His narrowed eyes were hard and filled with grim resolve as he helped Mary into her saddle.

"I wish you would give up on this," she murmured, her brows knit with worry. "We should just find another town. Abilene, perhaps, or Dodge City."

"No," was Luther's curt reply, and he climbed aboard his own horse. "I have a bone to pick with that damned cowboy. Besides, while I was in the saloon I found out about the woman he's riding with. Seems her father is a big rancher down in Texas. Or was. Wordis, he's dead. The Rocking Chair ranch. That means she's worth money."

Mary Keyes groaned softly. "We are going to follow them all the way to Texas? There are a lot of bad people in the Indian Territories, Luther. Your need for revenge is going to get us killed!"

Keyes glared at her. "Shut up, Mary. I just made us some money. Yeah, there are a lot of bad people in the Territories. But it's worth the risk. We'll make money off that woman. And I am going to kill that bastard Colbry."

He reined his horse around and rode deeper into the alley, then turned on the next street to the west to leave Ellsworth, his worried sister reluctantly following.

Chapter Six

The distance from Ellsworth to Lampasas, Texas was roughly six hundred miles. It had taken Colbry and the rest of the Rocking Chair cowboys over two months to get the Rocking Chair herd to the railhead. It took three weeks to ride back.

The journey was mostly uneventful. It seldom rained much in the Panhandle, where the Red River, which formed the border between Texas and the Indian Territories, originated, so the crossing was easy enough. They had no trouble with the bandits and renegades who help up trains and ambushed, robbed and sometimes murdered law-abiding folk who had to travel in other ways through the Territories.

Some of the Rocking Chair hands were taking one or two of their spare horses back with them. The others had sold their spares in Ellsworth. There were twenty ponies among them, and then the four mules that pulled the chuckwagon, which together made an attractive target for thieves and cutthroats. But renegades generally prowled alone, and bandit groups had a high attrition rate and seldom numbered more than three or four men. It didn't become less dangerous when they crossed the Red River, though. Comanches ranged far and wide, and every mile they traveled into Texas, the greater was the risk of running into them. And no sane person, except perhaps for scalp hunters, ever wanted to run into the Comanches.

Colbry thought that Laurie Ruston weathered the long ride very well. She didn't seem to mind the hardships of the trail. She was an excellent rider, and her thoroughbred was a strong, smooth ride with tremendous stamina. In night camps Laurie would sit around the campfire with the men and regale them with vivid tales of life in the east. She didn't talk much about her doings, but rather told amusing tales of politics, customs and fancy balls. She also regaled the cowboys with stories featuring her audience's favorite topic, women. It was a subject on which most of the men had limited experience. For their part, the cowboys told her funny or exciting tales of the frontier, some of which, assumed Colbry, were greatly embellished. Tall tales were commonplace in the west. Storytelling replaced literature where books were few and far between and a fair number of people couldn't read, and it behooved men to exaggerate their courage and their skill with weapons and horses in order to make others think twice about trying to take advantage of them.

The cowboys were also polite and, in some cases, downright shy in Laurie's presence. When she washed herself in a creek or river shallows, they gave her privacy and policed themselves. When one of them told a bawdy tale featuring a whore he had met in Ellsworth or some other wild and woolly cowtown, the others turned on him. Colbry noticed that they also tried very hard to be presentable, to look cleaner and smell better than range riders typically did. Based on the way they gazed at her, and how tongue-tangled they sometimes became when trying to talk to her, Colbry suspected that a fair number were smitten with her. It wasn't that any of them wanted to obtain ownership of the Rocking Chair brand through her. They weren't connivers. But range riding was a lonely profession and there were precious few upstanding and unmarried women around. Cowboys often wore their hearts on their sleeves. There was no question that she had won them over.

Emil Canfield seemed especially smitten. One day, as the sun was setting in a blaze of orange glory, Colbry was leading a saddleless Boots down to a rollicking creek a stone's throw from the night camp, intent on washing the dirt from two days' ride off the buckskin horse, when he spotted the young, lanky cowboy standing near some brush. Curious, Colbry bent his steps that way, Boots in tow. When he drew near he saw that Canfield was looking sheepish.

"What are you doing out here, Emil?"

"Well I…you see, I…" He half-turned and pointed back over his left shoulder. "Miss Ruston is a little further down the creek. She uh, well, she's washing up. I just figured I would, you know, watch out for her." Embarrassed, he turned quite pale and hastily added, "I ain't spying on her, Mr. Colbry! No, sir, not at all. But, well, it just don't seem safe for a woman to go off on her own in this country, especially at nightfall."

Colbry managed not to laugh, but he was grinning as he nodded, clapped Canfield's bony shoulder, and without another word towed Boots back to the spot further downstream that he had picked for the buckskin's wash.

For her part, Laurie did her fair share of work and more during the journey. She won Alonso over by refraining from even a suggestion that she assist him in the cooking, which the old Mexican would have taken as a slight. The cook, though, was happy to let her help wash dishes and she impressed him with her skill in handling and taking care of the mule team that pulled the chuckwagon. She slept on a blanket on the ground and never complained. Having purchased a Winchester .44 caliber Yellowboy rifle in Ellsworth, she proved she knew how to shoot when a five-foot diamondback rattler came out from under some brush and crossed their trail in front of her. Even though her thoroughbred balked and fiddle-footed, she pulled the Yellowboy out of the scabbard tied to her saddle and killed the aggressive snake with a single shot that separated its head from its body before Colbry could pull his Schofield pistol clear of its holster. It was either fine marksmanship or blind luck.

He complimented her that night as they sat around the campfire with the crew. "You shoot as well as your father did," he said.

She was leaning back, gazing up at the countless stars in the night sky, and didn't look his way when she replied. "He started teaching me when I was big enough to hold a rifle." Her tone was melancholy and Colbry wished he hadn't said anything, since it had conjured up a memory of John Ruston. "I seldom had the opportunity back east but I guess it's something you never forget how to do," she added.

They made good time down the old Chisholm Trail to Waco, and then crossed the Brazos River to head west by southwest toward Lampasas, three-days ride over pretty rugged country. By now all the cowboys were edgy because they were entering the heart of Comancheria. Colbry took it upon himself to ride a few miles ahead of the group, which was slowed down by the chuck wagon. He expected to see at least some sign of Comanche riders and before long he found some. Having tracked the Apaches, he could track just about anything, and he could read sign better than he could read the printed word. He figured that there were five braves on unshod ponies. It didn't alarm him. Five was enough to hit an isolated homestead or waylay a lone rider, but it wasn't likely they would attack a dozen Rocking Chair riders. He scanned the low rocky bluffs around him but didn't see anyone and didn't expect to. You rarely saw a Comanche until they were attacking you.

That night he doubled the guard around their camp and explained why. After supper, Laurie spoke up about the Indian sign.

"When I was a child I was never allowed to leave the ranch alone," she said. "In fact, I was rarely out of sight of the ranch house, and never without an escort. When we went to church in Lampasas, half the hands rode with us. And my father always tried to have two men together when they rode the range. Still, I remember that a couple of times a ranch hand disappeared." She looked away from the campfire to glance at Colbry. "The consensus was that the Comanches had ambushed and killed them. Their bodies were never found."

"You wouldn't have wanted to," drawled Burr Welken, laying on his blankets on the other side of the fire. When she looked his way, puzzled, he added "They strip their captives and stake 'em out, then skin 'em and slice the skin off 'em. They'll have their way with women and girls before they roast 'em alive."

"Burr," said Colbry curtly.

Burr sat up, wrapped his arms around his knees and looked at Colbry. "It's the cold, hard truth and she needs to know it. Pardon me, miss, but you were just a kid when you were last in these parts. You may have known such things but it's been many years since you were here and I wanted to make sure you know the risks."

Colbry glanced over at Laurie. She was solemn, but smiled and nodded at the Burr. "I know why you said it, and I appreciate it. I just don't know why they are so cruel."

"Some say they torture their captives to see just how courageous they are," said Colbry. The braver they are when they face certain death, the more credit the braves receive. But others say it's because they're hoping to discourage other white men from intruding on their land."

"Or, they could just be sadistic bastards," remarked a cowboy. "Whatever the truth of it is, if I never run into one it'll be too soon."

Alonso, busy at work at the chuckwagon, said, "I wish los demonios would just go away." He meant the Comanches. Just a mention of them rattled him.

"This was their land before we took it," remarked Burr. "And I reckon they will be around for a while longer. The army is of little use. And there are only a handful of Texas Rangers and that ain't enough to push the Comanches west. Just yet."

Laurie spoke up. "I never saw one and I'm thankful for that. The Lords of the Plains, isn't that what some folks call them? My father told me that they were responsible for driving the Spanish out. He also told me about the Fort Parker massacre. How they lured Ben Parker out using a white flag, which usually meant they wanted to trade. But once the gate was open they rushed in and killed almost everyone. They tied Parker down, skinned him, emasculated him, and then killed him. They pinned a woman to the ground with a spear and took turns violating her. They hauled off a woman and four children as slaves." She took a deep breath and let it out slowly, then looked over at Colbry. "But they won't run me off. And if it looks like they are going to capture me I'll kill myself, unless one of you are man enough to do it for me."

The cowboys were grimly silent, and for a moment the only sound was an owl hooting in the brush, the crackle of the fire, and the sounds of the horses on their line.

"We won't let that happen," said Colbry.

"Hell no, we won't," vowed Burr, grimly.

She looked at all the men around the fire and smiled. Colbry noticed the gratitude gleaming in her eyes. He studied the faces of the other men and saw that they were all impressed by Laurie Ruston's courage, and he was confident then that they would all lay down their lives for her if they had to. Smiling, he stretched out on his blankets and went to sleep.

The next day someone took a shot at him.

He was riding ahead of the others again, checking for sign, and was out in the great wide open when he heard the distinctive buzz of a bullet passing close by before he heard the report of the rifle that had fired it. Boots snorted and started to run; it was what his rider usually asked him to do when there was a gunshot. But Colbry checked him, pulling hard on the rein leather, and Boots locked his back legs and skidded to a stop. Colbry was already out of the saddle, and had pulled his 50-70 Sharps out of its boot on the way. It was the newest version of the rifle much used in the Civil War, and was favored by buffalo hunters and widely used by the U.S. Army on the frontier for its range and accuracy.

He slapped Boots on the rump and the buckskin took off, and then began circling around. Colbry didn't see this, but it was what the horse had been trained to do. Instead, Colbry threw himself on the ground and searched the high ridge some four hundred yards to the northwest, the general location from which the shot had come, because he had seen it kick up a little cloud of sand and rock splinters to his left. He couldn't see any rifle smoke so he tempted the shooter by rising up on one knee, the Sharps snug against his shoulder, and pulled up the back sight. He didn't see anything moving on the skyline but he didn't expect to. So he made a rough guess based on what he had heard and seen of the first round fired at him and squeezed the trigger. Then he half-cocked the carbine, opened the breech and replaced the spent shell with a fresh round. He carried six of the rounds in his gunbelt, with more in his saddlebags. He aimed a little to the left of his first shot and fired again. This time he saw movement, two figures coming up off the ground to move away from the edge. Colbry pushed a third round into the breech, closed it, cocked the carbine, took quick aim and fired a third time. One of the figures went down, to be helped up by the other man. Colbry got off a fourth shot before they disappeared.

He lay still for a moment, then heard Boots coming up behind him. Getting to his feet, Colbry sheathed the reloaded Sharps and, keeping his eye on the ridge, climbed into the saddle. He was certain that he had hit one of the men, whom he assumed were Comanches. Riding east, back toward the rest of his party, he kept an eye on the ridgeline until he was a half mile away and his nerves had settled.

When he rejoined the others it was Welken who could look at the expression on his face and note the dirt and dust on his clothes and asked, "What did you run into, Cord?"

"Couple of Comanche scouts, I think, but too far away to be sure. One of them took a shot at me. Saw two of them but could've been more. I think maybe I winged one." He looked around at the concerned faces of Laurie and the rest of the cowboys. "I want two men to ride point with me for a while. The ones I saw may be part of a larger band nearby, and they may show up again to even the score."

"I'll go," said Welken, a gleam in his eye and a grimace on his gaunt, weathered face.

"Me too," said Emil Caulfield.

Colbry almost told Caulfield no. He was just a kid, after all. But then he thought twice about it and nodded. He wasn't doing the kid any favors by coddling him. "We'll ride a hundred yards apart. Burr, you ride a hundred yards to my left. Caulfield, you stay a hundred yards to the left of him." He looked grimly at Laurie. "I want you to stay alongside the chuck wagon on the left side. I don't want them to see you or that horse you ride. If they do, they might well come a-running. And if they do that, you get into the wagon pronto. Understand?"

Laurie heard the steel in his voice, and saw the determined look on his face and just nodded. A little surprised that she didn't object to leaving Beholden and hiding from danger, Colbry climbed into Boot's saddle and rode west with Welken and Caulfield. They passed the point where he had been ambushed. Curiosity got the better of him and he found a way up onto the low ridge and checked for sign and finally found some. He counted three riders on unshod horses and wearing moccasins. At least they weren't Apaches, he thought. Tracking Apaches was the hardest thing he had ever had to do..

As a line rider, Colbry knew where the open range ended and Laurie Ruston's property began, even though there were no fences on the eastern boundary. When he was a couple of miles away from the ranch house, he and his companions paused in the shade of a few cottonwoods lining a dry ravine and waited for the rest of the party to reach him. An hour later they arrived at the ranch house.

John Ruston had built it like a fortress of adobe and sandstone. It was sixty-feet square, two stories tall, with a large gate for a front door. Inside, a dozen rooms overlooked a courtyard of gray granite stones. Each room had gunports on its outer wall. There were twelve-pane windows with interior shutters in the walls overlooking the courtyard. There was a main room on the first floor on the southern side, where John Ruston had his office and a big comfortably furnished space for entertaining guests in front of a big fireplace. There was a kitchen, Alonso's domain, and a large storage room on the west side, and across from the main room, on the northern side, was a dining room and a reading room, its walls lined with bookcases burdened with more books than Colbry had seen collected in one place. On the second floor were four bedrooms, each with its own stone fireplace, the largest above the main room and sporting its own bath. Across from it were two more bedrooms and on the western side a separate room with a bath, a small storage area. A narrow staircase was on the western side. This led one to the flat rooftop, with a knee-high crenelated wall all the way around The house had withstood tornadoes and several large-scale attacks by Comanches and the Comachero bandits led by the infamous Juan Secudo ten years ago in retribution for Ruston's raid on one of their rendezvous sites, this after they began to buy stolen Rocking Chair cattle from their Comanche associates. But by the time Colbry arrived on the scene, there had not been an attack on this fortress home for years.

The outbuildings included a large barn, stable, tack house and wellhouse, surrounded by a half dozen corrals. And there was a graveyard ringed by a pole fence. Colbry thought it likely John Ruston was buried there, and glanced at Laurie. She had seen the cemetery too and her gaze was bleak, but apparently was content to wait until later to visit her father's final resting place, perhaps when she could be alone.

A few stalwart oak and cedar trees offered some shade from the blistering hot summer sun. Colbry imagined that there had once been many more trees, but they had been cut down to provide a good view all around, for defensive purposes. Gently rolling land carpeted with tall yellowing grass stretched in all directions. A line of trees a few hundred yards to the south marked the course of a rocky creek.

Someone at the ranch house spotted the little caravan and began ringing a bell. The big gate had been swung open by a vaquero by the time Colbry and the others had neared the house, and they entered the courtyard. A few curious cowboys who had been working around the barn and corrals followed them in. Trace Simmons emerged from the main room. He was a large, broad-shouldered man with dark brown eyes in a square-jawed face and coal-black hair under his hat. In addition to his side gun, he had a Bowie knife, in a leather sheath, stuck under his wide leather belt. Selman was a self-important man who was inclined to remind the hands of his authority when it wasn't necessary, and Colbry was thankful that as a linerider he hadn't seen much of the man or felt the brunt of his overbearing manner.

Colbry looked over at Laurie and pointed at him. "There's your foreman," he said. Laurie turned Beholden that way and he followed suit, dismounting so he could take her reins while she climbed down out of her saddle, then tied Boots and Beholden to the nearest hitching post. The chuck wagon circled around the exterior of the ranch house, where a back door to Alonso's kitchen was located. Welken, Caulfield, and the rest of the men who had been on the cattle drive dismounted and hitched their horses near the adjacent bunkhouse. Some of them responded to greetings from those of their brethren who had stayed behind. Burr and Emil and a couple of others trailed Laurie and Colbry into the ranch house courtyard.

Laurie went up to Simmons and extended a hand. "Mr. Simmons. My name is Laurie Ruston, John's daughter."

Surprised, Simmons stared at her, then at Colbry, then back at Laurie, and swept the hat off his head.

"Mr. Ruston had told me to send word to you if anything happened to him. I did that, but I never heard back. I for sure didn't expect you to come all this way."

"Why wouldn't I?" she asked, still smiling, with a curious tilt of her head. "This is my father's dream come true. And it's my birthplace. I vividly remember playing with my father's hunting hounds, and how he taught me how to ride and shoot." She looked around the courtyard. "I don't see them. The hounds."

"The dogs are gone," replied Simmons, gruffly. "Guess I figured you'd want to sell the Rocking Chair. I mean this ain't no place for a lady. I've already heard from a few men who are interested in buying it. One of them is Barrett Faulkner, the owner of the Elmwood ranch. His spread is south of here."

"This is my birthplace, Mr. Simmons. And my birthright. With the help of Mr. Colbry and these men and yourself, I intend to keep my father's dream alive."

Simmons looked at Colbry. "What happened to the rest of the crew that rode with you?"

"When they found out about Big John's death, a few of them wanted to split the proceeds from the sale of the herd and ride on," replied Colbry. "But I wanted no part of that and had a bit of trouble with Tom Selman. So he and the others went their own way."

Simmons looked around. Some of the cowboys were near enough to overhear the conversation. "I reckon some of these boys might not cotton to working for a woman, either," he said.

"Does that include you, Mr. Simmons?" asked Laurie with a polite but humorless smile.

Simmons ran blunt fingers through coal-black hair as he thought about it. Then he called out to the rest of the Rocking Chair cowboys within earshot and told them to gather round. He waited until they had come closer before he spoke.

"Some of you already know this is John Ruston's daughter. Some of you don't. She owns the Rocking Chair now. If anyone has a problem with that, take a day to think it through then tell me so, and if you want to find greener pastures you'll be paid what you're owed and sent on your way. That's all."

"No, it isn't." Laurie turned from watching Ruston to face the cowboys gathered around behind her. "I wish for all of you to continue riding for the brand. It's true, I was sent east when I was very young. But I was born and raised here, and I want the Rocking Chair to be the best cattle ranch it can be. For that, I need your help. If I tell you to do something that you don't think is in the best interests of the ranch then I want you to tell me so. But with the advice of Mr. Simmons and Mr. Colbry, I hope that will seldom if ever happen. So think about it, talk it over amongst yourselves. It's entirely your choice, of course."

The cowboys looked at one another and then wandered off with some muted conversation.

"How did my father die, Mr. Simmons?" asked Laurie.

"Sometimes he would take a ride. He always wanted to go off on his own. Can't say as to why."

"I think I do," she replied. "Sometimes you have to get away from the burden of responsibility. The land can remind you why you took that burden on."

"I reckon you want to come inside," said Simmons, brows knit, clearly unable to fully comprehend what she was talking about. He turned and opened the door he had just passed through. Laurie thanked him and entered, and Colbry followed, taking off his hat. As soon as he crossed the threshold Simmons fastened his dark gaze on him and said, "I'll be wanting you back on the line. And take another man. With Comanches and those damn rustlers around, no one rides alone."

Taken by surprise, Laurie turned and looked at Colbry with dismay. "I think... "

"I'll be going," said Colbry, putting his hat back on and then touching the brim with a smile. He had a hunch that now was not the time for Laura to override her foreman. "Good luck. I'll be seeing you around."

Before she could reply, he was through the door and had closed it behind him. He saw Emil Caulfield leading his horse out of the courtyard and called to him, then crossed the hardpack to the young cowboy.

"You're coming with me, Emil," he said.

"Where to?"

"The western line shack."

"Why not me?" asked Welken, having overheard. "That's maybe the most dangerous place on the Rocking Chair right now, and Emil here is hardly more than a tenderfoot." He glanced at his young friend and added, " Sorry, Emil, but it's true, and the western line is one-eye-always-open territory."

"Well, for one thing, because he needs to learn how to read sign, and I reckon I might be able to teach him," said Colbry.

"You know more about it than anyone riding for the brand," admitted Burr, "seeing as how you can track an ant over a rock."

Colbry turned to Emil. "Bring an extra horse out of the remuda, while I go get some supplies from Alonso." When Emil, who appeared excited by the prospect of riding the line, was out of earshot, Colbry said to Burr, "Do me a favor. Keep an eye on Miss Ruston."

Burr smiled and clapped him on the shoulder. "You can count on it. She doesn't strike me as a woman Trace can ride roughshod over, but there's no telling. He might give it a whirl." He turned to lead his horse to a corral and some grain and a long drink of trough water. "Keep your hair on, Cord!" he called over his shoulder.

The sun was nearing the western horizon when Luther Keyes and his sister rode up to a cabin deep in the thickets close by the Arkansas River in the Indian Territories. Traveling through the rough country had been arduous, and Keyes had lost his way a time or two, with only the sunrise and the sunset keeping them more or less heading south. The Keyes were tired and dirty when they spotted the cabin. It had been another long day as both of them fretted about running into renegade Indians or outlaws. The cabin was a run-down structure and Luther thought at first that it might be uninhabited, until he saw three horses and a mule in a ramshackle corral behind it. By then it was too late to slip away. Three men emerged from the cabin. One of them had a double-barrel shotgun in hand. The other two had pistols stuck in their belts. The first man kept a wary eye on Luther, while the others gaped at Mary, who looked like she would have much preferred being absolutely anywhere else.

Luther Keyes had a bad feeling, and his smile was taut as he nodded at the men. The one with the shotgun sauntered closer and grinned a nearly toothless grin at the gambler. His two companions were looking at Mary the way starving men would stare at food.

"What are you doing out this way, mister?" asked the shotgun toter.

"Just passing through. On our way to Texas."

"Texas, you say. Well, you're a long way from Texas, friend." The man glanced over at Mary. "This your wife?"

"My sister. We're sorry to bother you. We'll be moving on."

One of the other men had moved closer to Mary's horse, and he fingered the fabric of her riding skirt, then began to lift it up to catch a glimpse of her leg. Mary jerked on the reins and her mount snorted and began fiddle-footing. The third man lunged forward and grabbed the bridle.

"We got room to spare, and some food," said the shotgunner. "You two are welcome to stay here tonight. We sure wouldn't mind some company, would we, boys?"

The one with the grip on Mary's bridle chuckled. "No sirree, we wouldn't mind, Jake. This woman does smell better than you do."

Luther was pushing back his coat to reach for the pistol in his belt, but the one named Joe saw the movement and brought the shotgun up and growled, "I wouldn't do that if I were you, pilgrim. Now, slow and easy, bring it out with two fingers and drop it." When Luther did as he was told, Joe kicked the pistol away. "Now, get down off that horse."

Dismounting, Luther held his hands up in hopes of putting Joe at ease. "We don't want any trouble, mister."

Joe chuckled. "Then you shouldn't have come here." He glanced over his shoulder at his two cohorts. "Boys, why don't you take the little lady inside and show her some hospitality."

Mary looked at Luther, eyes widening with a terrified realization of what the men intended. With Joe's attention elsewhere for an instant, Luther lunged into him, leading with a shoulder and grabbing for the barrels of the shotgun, shouting, "Ride, Mary! Get out of..."

Joe was quick to react, sidestepping, and slammed the butt of the shotgun against the side of Luther's head and knocked him to the ground. With a cry of despair, Mary wrenched on her reins, trying to turn the horse under her. But the man with a grip on the bridle held on and dug his heels in, pulling the mount's head down, while the other man grabbed Mary's leg and pulled her roughly off the saddle. She landed poorly and lay there, stunned for an instant, the wind knocked out of her. When she started to get up, one the man who had yanked her out of the saddle put a pistol to her head.

"Why don't you come along inside and accept our hospitality?" asked the man, and then leered at Joe. "Been a long time since I've had me a white woman."

Luther managed to sit up, blood matting his hair. His world was spinning but he managed to stammer, "Wait...please. I—I came here looking for help."

Joe was startled, then skeptical. "Help? What the hell for?"

"You know the name John Ruston?"

"Sure. He owns one of the biggest spreads in Texas."

"He did. He's dead. But he has a daughter. She came home from somewhere back East to take over the ranch."

Joe frowned. "What the hell does that have to do with us?"

"She's worth many thousands of dollars." His mind racing, Luther tried to read Joe's grizzled face. He could tell that the other man was puzzled. He glanced across at

Mary and saw the terror on her dusty, tear-streaked face and came up with a story he thought might appeal to these men. "I plan to kidnap her, hold her for ransom." He looked up at Joe again. "But I need help. Your help. We'll get more money than we could make off with by holding up a bank. And we can split it, me, you and your friends. Equal shares."

Joe scowled at him, and for a moment Luther thought the other man wasn't going to buy into his story. But then Joe rested the shotgun on his shoulder and rubbed his grizzled chin.

"You expect we could go up against a whole ranch crew?"

Luther's mind was racing. He hadn't had the leisure to think everything through. "Listen to me," he said, buying a little time to think of a good answer. "She came home from somewhere back east when her father died. She brought a thoroughbred horse with her. A horse that means everything to her. We steal the horse and then we let her know we'll kill it if she doesn't pay a ransom. She'll pay up. And when she does, your men grab her. Then we have the ransom and the horse." He glanced at Joe's cohorts. "And we have her. We keep all three."

Joe glanced at his compadres. One of them whined, "Oh come on, Joe." He tangled his fingers in Mary's hair. "Let's have some fun."

"Shuddup!" growled Joe. "I'm tryin' to think."

Luther decided it was time for him to go all in. "What do you get if you kill us? Two horses and some tack. We have no money. And after you kill us you'll still be stone broke. I've seen John Ruston's daughter, in Ellsworth. She's young and pretty." He glanced at his sister, hoping that Mary still had her wits about her and that she wouldn't let slip that they had never talked about any of the story he was telling. For one thing they had never laid eyes on Ruston's daughter. "I've seen the thoroughbred she brought with her, too. He's worth thousands of dollars. So all we have to do is slip in and steal that horse. We won't have to face down a bunch of cowboys."

A grin slowly creased Joe's face. "You're a smart one. Maybe we can do business together."

"But, Joe…" whined one of the others.

"Shut the hell up!"

"If we pull this off you'll have enough money to buy the services of a high-priced whore every day of the week and twice on Sundays," said Luther, speaking not just to Joe but the other two, as well.

Joe walked over to Mary, bent over to latch onto one of her arms, and pulled her to her feet. Then he told one of his partners to get some rope before turning to Luther.

"We're going to tie you both up, just in case you're spinning a yarn. When I see this thoroughbred you speak of, then I'll cut you loose and we can partner up."

Luther didn't have to think it over. Being a captive trumped being dead. "That's fine," he said, "but there's one other thing. If you harm a hair on my sister's head, the deal is off."

Joe snorted his derision. "What makes you think my boys and I couldn't pull this off all by our lonesome?"

"Because I know one of the men who works for her. He'll help us. But he won't help you without me."

Mary looked at him with wide-eyed shock. But Joe didn't see that. He was focused on Luther, his mind racing. Then he grinned at Luther, while speaking to one of his partners. "Jed, go inside and make a fresh pot of brown gargle. Frank, take our new friends' horses over to the corral and give 'em some hay." He extended a hand to Luther. "Sorry for hitting you upside the head ... partner."

Luther took the proffered hand, and once he was on his feet and certain he wouldn't fall down again, he muttered, "Don't mention it."

CHAPTER SEVEN

It was a day's ride to the western line cabin and when Colbry and Emil Caulfield arrived, the sun was setting in their eyes, painting the pale-blue western sky with bold strokes of bright orange and rosy red. Colbry saw some sign of Comanches and pointed it out to the young cowboy riding with him, explaining how to estimate how long ago the Indians had passed that way and in which direction they were traveling. One set was only a day old, and the Indians were heading north by west. Going home, Colbry reckoned, heading back to Comancheria, which included most of West Texas, and probably carrying loot, and maybe even captives women and children, after conducting a raid. He couldn't help but wonder about the death and misery they had caused. He didn't hate them, as many Texans did. The Comanches were aggressively trying to stop the slow but relentless westward spread of the white man. They were trying to protect their loved ones, their lands, and their way of life. He understood them. But he also understood that ultimately they would fail. Many on both sides would have to die before that happened.

The line shack was hidden in scrub brush on high ground, a small, well-made cabin fashioned from square-cut timber and stone. There was a small corral nearby. Water was nearly a mile away, a natural spring. The shack wasn't built near the water source because the Comanches and probably some bandidos to boot, knew of the spring and could be expected to show up there from time to time. There were a bunch of waterskins in the cabin, and Colbry told his companion that they would ride to the spring the next day to fill them up.

The interior of the shack measured about twelve feet by fifteen, big enough for two over and under bunks, a table, two chairs and a barrel to sit on, a small stove, smaller supply barrels and some shelves secured to the walls laden with sacks containing such staples as cornmeal, salt, flour and some jerked meat. There were canisters with sugar, coffee beans, yeast and other luxuries. The roof was fairly new; this Colbry knew because he had been one of the men who repaired it after a tornado had ripped much of it away the summer before. It didn't look like anyone had visited the cabin, much less helped themselves to the provisions since last he had been there, some three months ago.

Colbry was too tired to do much more than make some coffee and settle down at the table to drink a cup. He and Emil had taken care of their horses and put them in the corral in the darkening dusk and it was full night before they could finally take their ease. Emil helped himself to some jerky and a hardtack biscuit, which he was wise enough to inspect for weevils. He took stock of rolls of barbed wire and the tools used to put it up that were stashed in one corner of the room.

"How long is the western fence?" he asked Colbry.

"Fifteen miles or so. It's about a thousand yards west of us. We'll ride south tomorrow and look for gaps after we fetch fresh water. Sometimes Comanches tear down a section. Sometimes it's the weather. And sometimes it's rustlers, too."

"What keeps them from tearing it down again after we fix it?"

Colbry smiled faintly. "That would be us. If we see the fence down in the same place two or three times, we'll make camp nearby and wait for the chance to discourage whoever's doing the damage."

Emil was silent for a moment, deep in thought. Colbry surmised the young man was thinking about facing down wild Indians and desperadoes. Then Emil asked, "Have you had many dust ups riding the line?"

"I've had a few."

"Bunkhouse talk is that you used to fight Apaches."

"As seldom as I could. But yeah, I tracked them for the army."

"I've heard stories about the Apaches. The Comanches, too." Emil was leaning forward, elbows on the table, slowly rubbing his hands together, a worried expression on his face. "I hear if they take you captive you'll be a long time dying. I remember what you said about them, why they are the way they are, that night when we were coming back from Ellsworth with Miss Ruston?"

Colbry nodded. "They want everyone to fear them. To stay away. They don't want to end up like the tribes back east."

"Do you? Fear them, I mean."

Colbry thought about that for a moment, then shook his head. "No. Because if you do you might make a mistake. You might hesitate. Second-guess yourself." He realized he was trying to explain how he could stifle emotion when it came to a dangerous situation, how he could become a "cold-blooded killer" as an army lieutenant in Apacheria had once labeled him.

The young cowboy grimaced. "I don't know how brave I could be," He admitted.

"You don't think about it, you just do it."

Emil was taken aback by the quiet ferocity with which Colbry spoke those words, while Colbry regretted his tone of voice. For his part, Emil fell silent for a moment, pondering. I ain't never killed anybody," he admitted.

Colbry nodded. He knew what Emil was going through. Not just the fear of his own death, but uncertainty with regard to his grit when it came down to killing or being killed.

"That's nothing to be ashamed of. Hope you never have to."

Emil nodded, forcing a wan smile onto his lips. "I guess you have."

"Once or twice. Most of the time you don't have a choice unless you're ready to die."

"How many men have you killed, Cord?"

Colbry shook his head. "Too many. Not proud of any of it."

"Were you scared?"

"Don't wait for that. You'll know what you have to do to keep from dying and you just do it." Colbry looked down at the cup cradled in his hands. "And I try not to think about it too much afterward. I don't wonder if there was a way out of killing. You can't think like that. You don't have to if the only option to killing someone is to die yourself." He studied Emil's expression as the latter fell silent and looked inward, wondering if he had what it took to survive on the frontier. "What made you decide to be a cowboy?" asked Colbry, intentionally changing the subject.

The young man shrugged and Colbry could tell that Emil was self-conscious talking about himself. "My pa owned a general store down Nacogdoches way, and my brother and I were supposed to inherit it. My brother was happy to follow in pa's footsteps. I wasn't. I wanted ..." He hesitated, searching for the right word.

"Adventure?" suggested Colbry.

"Yeah, that, I guess." Emil shrugged again. "I sure didn't want to be a store clerk my whole life. So one day I just up and rode west. I was lucky. Mr. Ruston found me before the Comanches did and gave me a job. Said he admired my spunk, riding alone and all."

Colbry smiled. "He was a good judge of character."

Emil looked at him, flattered and surprised. He mumbled an embarrassed thanks, then murmured, "I think sometimes it was more foolishness than bravery." He paused, then asked, "Mr. Colbry, The Good Book says thou shalt not kill. It's right there in the Commandments. If I have to kill a man, even in self-defense, am I going to Hell?"

Colbry rose and headed for the door, grabbing his Sharps rifle. His expression was bleak. "If it ever comes down to having to kill another man, pray for forgiveness. And if that doesn't work, I guess I'll meet you in Hell. Now I'm gonna take a look around. You should get some sleep. It's gonna be a long day tomorrow."

They were in the saddle before daybreak and rode to the spring with all the waterskins tied to their rigs, filled the skins and then returned to the line shack. They didn't linger there; there were hours of light left and Colbry wanted to ride the line. Within an hour they found a section of the fence down. The sign was clear enough. The wire had been cut and about fifty cattle had been moved off Ruston land by three men on horseback. The horses were shod. Emil asked Colbry if it had been Indians who had done the rustling.

"Now and then they do. But they rarely ride shod horses."

They rode on across the rolling prairie, following the tracks. As Colbry had expected, they found an abandoned camp about ten miles further southwest. He dismounted, handing his reins to Emil, and told the young cowboy to dismount, since he made less of a target out of the saddle, then spent a few minutes walking around, studying the ground. When he returned, there was a frown on his lean, weathered face.

"They camped here for the night. Definitely white men. Comanches don't wear boots. This morning they turned south."

A few hours later they were traveling on a ledge alongside a ravine when Colbry abruptly checked Boots and held up a hand for Emil to pull up. Then he pointed to the ground.

"They pushed the cattle into the ravine," he said, then put his buckskin horse into motion again, keeping to the high ground. The ravine widened and before long he stopped again and told Emil to listen. They could hear cattle in distress up ahead, accompanied by men shouting. Colbry dismounted, pulled his Sharps long gun out of its saddle boot and led his horse a little deeper into the brush. A hundred feet further on, he ground-hitched Boots and motioned for Emil to follow him as he proceeded on foot. A few minutes later they were looking down into the ravine from the cover of a bunch of sage.

The Rocking Chair cattle were there, kept clumped together by several men on horseback while two more hands were stretching a cow out on its side and two more men were at a fire. They watched a man leave the fire with a branding iron in hand, and then burn the brand on the cow's flank.

Colbry recognized him. It was Tom Selman, the cowboy he had fought at the Ellsworth train station.

"Isn't that…" began Emil, then shut his mouth when Colbry put a finger to his own lips. But Emil was agitated, and couldn't keep quiet for long. "Shouldn't we…"

This time Colbry gave him an angry look and clamped a hand around the breech of the young cowboy's rifle. He had already decided that, as much as he wanted to put a bullet in Selman, he couldn't risk it. The odds were six against two. He might have decided to take them down if he had been accompanied by Burr Welken, but Emil was green around the gills. He couldn't be sure that the youngster would be of much use in a shootout, and he didn't want to get him killed. He gestured for the kid to follow him and slowly backed away from the rim of the ledge. Nary a word passed between them until they reached their horses, then Colbry told Emil to mount up and led the way eastward, the linerider cabin their destination.

Colbry didn't sleep much that night, trying to decide if he should return to the ranch house and inform Laurie Ruston of what they had found out, or send Emil. The next morning, over a breakfast of bacon and sourdough biscuits, he told the young cowboy that he was going to ride back to give the news to Laurie.

"That means you're going to be on your own for a day or two," he said. "But I figure you can handle things. Get to work on fixing that fence. You've got everything you need here. If you see anyone, you ride like hell back here and stay inside until I, or someone else, comes to help."

"Don't worry," replied Emil, "I can handle it." He smiled, grateful that Colbry thought enough of him to leave him on his own with a big job to do.

Colbry nodded, hurried through the breakfast and minutes later was in the saddle and riding eastward.

It was still daylight when Colbry reached the Rocking Chair ranch headquarters. He spotted Laurie Ruston, dressed in much the same way as when he had first seen her on the steps of Ellsworth's Drovers Cottage. She was watching a cowboy trying to break a chestnut horse in one of the pens, with Burr Welken beside her and doing likewise. When Welken heard a rider coming up, he turned to look, then said something to Laurie, who looked around and smiled warmly.

Colbry climbed down out of the saddle, and tried to brush some of the dust and dirt off his shirt as the two approached him. It was obvious by the expression on her face that Laurie was happy to see him. Welken wore a concerned frown on his craggy, sun-whacked face. He could take one look at Colbry and see that there was trouble.

"What happened, Cord?" asked Burr.

"Rustlers. They cut the wire and made off with about fifty head of cattle."

The smile vanished from Laurie's face. "You know who did the deed?"

Colbry nodded. "They were cowboys. And one of them was Tom Selman."

Laurie and Welken exchanged glances.

"How do you know that?" she asked.

"Because I saw them."

"Did you kill him and get our cattle back?" asked Welken.

Colbry shook his head. "Nope."

"Why the hell not?"

Laurie was studying Colbry's grim visage and said, "Because of Emil Caulfield. Isn't that right, Cord?"

"Yep. That's right."

Welken grimaced. "If you ask me, you should've gunned 'em down, Cord. Emil's got to learn sooner or later what it's like when men start slinging lead."

Colbry shook his head again. "No. There were seven of them. Even if it had been you and me, we could have gotten the short end of that stick."

"He's right," Laurie told Burr, then turned to Colbry. "You did the right thing. So what do you think they're going to do with our stock?"

He didn't miss the "our" stock comment or its implications, and admired Laurie all the more for saying it. She wanted the men working for her to feel as though they had a stake in the Rocking Chair Ranch, "I'm not sure. But they were branding them. And they were heading south."

Welken grunted. Many of the Rocking Chair cattle weren't branded, and wouldn't be until next spring, when it was time to drive a herd to market. "My money is on Barrett Faulkner," he said.

"Who is Barrett Faulkner?" asked Laurie.

"He showed up in these parts about fifteen years ago," replied Burr. "You weren't around then, were you? Your father had already sent you east. Faulkner carved out a spread south of the Rocking Chair. He didn't much care for John Ruston. Jealousy, I suspect. Faulkner is an ambitious man. He wants to be the top dog around here. Some folks say he owns Ben Mackey, the town sheriff of Lampasas. Wouldn't surprise me if he decided to help himself to our livestock once your father passed away."

Colbry studied Laurie's pretty face and was pleased to see the grim determination in her expression. He said, "Wouldn't be easy to change the Rocking Chair brand. If what we saw is the work of Faulkner, it's likely he keeps the unbranded cattle for himself and sells off the rest to people who wouldn't care if they were buying stolen beef. "Steals a few hundred cows, enough to make it worth the time and effort to push them down to the border and sell them, most likely to the Comancheros."

"We don't even know how many cattle we have, do we?" asked Laurie/.

"No, ma'am, not for sure," said Burr. "My best guess is somewhere six-seven hundred and a thousand right now. This spread is too big to know for certain. Every spring we round up hundreds to move them north to the railhead, and that's when we brand the ones we missed the year before."

Laurie pondered that for a moment, then smiled faintly at Colbry. "I want to go for a ride tomorrow if the weather allows. I would like for you to ride with me, and we can talk more about this problem."

Colbry glanced at Burr, who raised an amused eyebrow.

"Don't you think I should get back to the line shack?" asked Colbry. "Emil is by himself."

"Burr can take care of that, can't you, Burr?"

"Yes, ma'am!" said Welken, enthusiastically.

Colbry had mixed feelings. Part of him was happy to spend more time with Laurie Ruston. But he didn't like to be singled out in this way. It could result in his being hazed by some of the other hands because of it. Still, she was the boss, and he gave her a nod.

"I'll be ready at first light," he said.

⚜ ⚜ ⚜

They rode out at dawn, Laurie astride her black stallion, Colbry on Boots, who was always ready to travel, and headed north by west, across rolling, grassy hills, through thick stands of oaks, blackhaw and hawthorn along the rocky creek beds. Checking the stallion in the speckled shade of a small stand of post oaks less than an hour from the house, she pointed down into a long grassy valley ahead.

"Look there!" she exclaimed, delighted.

It was a herd of at least sixty wild horses gathered in the vicinity of a stream that meandered down the middle of the valley, about four hundred yards away. The wind was blowing in from the west, so the presence of two humans had not yet been detected.

Colbry was pleased to see them, but not surprised. This northern part of the Rocking Chair spread consisted of rolling hills with a lot of brush, interspersed with a few valleys such as the one below, but not much water. Most of the cattle were found to the south, but mustangs favored more remote areas. They were the feral descendants of horses brought north by Spanish conquistadors and were surefooted, sturdy, quick and wary.

Laurie looked over at him. "What do you see down there?"

"Well, they're fast and can run all day. They can be hard to handle and hard to break. They aren't partial to giving up their freedom any more than we are."

"Can you catch some for me?"

"I reckon so. But why? Most cowboys want to find and break their own."

"I want a dozen or so good mares."

He looked at her for a moment, then at the thorough-bred who wore her saddle. "You want to breed them," he said.

"Yes, that's right." She reached over and grabbed his arm. "There are dozens of cattle ranches in Texas, tens of thousands of cattle. The cattle business is going to be the lifeblood of this state for decades to come and it's going to spread even further west, despite the Comanches. And what do you need to raise cattle, besides land and water and drovers?"

Colbry returned his gaze to the distant herd of mustangs. "Horses," he said.

She nodded. "And not just any horses. The best that there can be." She leaned forward and stroked Beholden's neck. "We have the potential to do this, right here. Bring me at least a dozen mares, Cord."

Colbry thought it over and nodded. "You'll need eight to ten men, good riders who have fast horses and who are highly skilled with a lariat."

"You choose the men," said Laurie. "Just get me those mares."

Chapter Eight

The following day at dawn Colbry rode away from the ranch house with ten men he had hand-picked without even talking to them about the task in hand. Having been until recently a line rider, he didn't know many of the Rocking Chair hands very well and couldn't call them friends. He had done his part during the cattle roundup in the spring and he had seen how most of them had done their jobs on the cattle push, knew how they took care of their horses, their tack, and themselves, and also knew that they had some horse smarts.

A couple of days later they discovered a likely place to trap a herd of mustangs, a rocky gorge that narrowed on the western end. It took an entire day and most of another to fell some trees and gather some brush to close off the narrow end and, on the other end, to build the funnel, log fencing on either side and covered with brush that fanned out from the entrance to the gulch for about two hundred feet. The mouth of the funnel was about sixty yards wide.

Later that day they found the mustang herd, and began to follow it. The mustangs traveled ahead of them but the cowboys kept their distance and pace, following fresh horse manure when they lost sight of the herd. Once or twice a day the wild horses would circle around and come up on one side or the other of the cowboys and watch the riders warily. It was easy enough to pick out the herd's leader, a gray stallion with a black mane who kept apart from the others and often circled around the herd.

Colbry knew that mustangs were insatiably curious beasts. They were quick and alert and if he and his bunch charged at them they would bolt and, if pressed, might scatter. On the third day they managed to get within a few hundred yards of the wild ones. Colbry and some of the other men began grunting softly. The first time this happened the gray whinnied and every last one of his followers looked up and watched the cowboys intently, nostrils flaring. Suddenly the gray roared and galloped straight at the cowboys, then abruptly stopped and tossed its head, the long mane waving like a banner of war, unshod hooves stamping. Some of the herd's stallions followed him and did likewise. The gray stallion then became quite still, staring at the horsemen. Abruptly he began to jump and prance around and around, snorting violently. It was a magnificent display designed to demonstrate his fury and fearlessness, and the cowboys were impressed. A few minutes later the gray and his fellow stallions returned to the herd, which had already begun to move away.

The next day, the cowboys moved around to the north of the herd, which caused the herd to begin moving south by west, since they were drifting further and further away from the gulch and the brush corral. By this time the mustangs had become accustomed to their presence. The cowboys proceeded to make a little more noise, hooting and hollering now and then. Colbry knew that mustangs were as brave as men could be. They didn't spook or shy away from sudden loud noises, but would if someone or something suddenly and silently appeared and startled them. An hour before full dusk, Colbry gathered up the cowboys and left the herd, leaving one man to trail them from a distance.

Excitement was high in the cowboy camp that night. They ate jerky and hardtack, as there was no fire allowed, and if they spoke at all it was in hushed tones. As they ate, Colbry explained what lay ahead in considerable detail. After the sudden disappearance of their cowboy escort, the mustangs had stopped moving at sundown and were gathered about a third of a mile away near a small spring-fed stream. The corral in the gulch was less than a mile further out.

It was a clear night, without much wind, the moon casting night shadows. After eating, most of the men lay in their bedrolls, and most sooner or later got some sleep. Colbry stayed wide awake, listening to the night sounds. He was accustomed to sleepless nights and occupied himself with thoughts of Laurie Ruston, remembering their first meeting at The Drovers Cottage, how she had cared for him after the fight with Selman, and how she had won over the Rocking Chair cowboys during the long ride from Ellsworth. She wanted a dozen mares and he was going to do everything in his power to give her what she wanted.

A few hours later, Colbry picked eight men and sent them out. They slipped quietly into the night. Four of them would position themselves to one side of the mustang herd and four on the other. They had to be deathly quiet so as not to spook the herd, and would position themselves about fifty yards apart from one another and twice that far away from the wild horses.

About midnight, Colbry and the other two cowboys saddled up and slowly rode after the mustangs. It was easy enough, in the moonlight, to stay right on their tracks. They stopped a couple of hundred yards away from the herd. The night was quiet enough for them to hear the huffing and occasional whinny from the horses as a few coyotes sang to the waning moon way off in the distance. Colbry and the men with him dismounted and waited, reins in hand.

It was a couple of hours more when the sky began to lighten in the east. Still the cowboys waited. Right before the morning sun peeked over the horizon the cowboys mounted up and began their hooting. As far as Colbry was concerned, this was the key moment. They had to make sure the mustangs stayed on course, south by west, toward the gulch a mile away. The cowboys riding on both flanks began to veer slowly but steadily in on the herd, while Colbry and his companions urged their ponies into a lope. Before long the gulch lay just ahead. It was the moment of truth.

The cowboys spurred their ponies and began to holler, and whoop and a thunder rose from the ground, the thunder of hooves, as the mustangs bolted into a full-out gallop. The sun was perched on the eastern horizon now, blinding the horses that looked behind them. The herd charged down into the wide ravine that prefaced the gulch. Colbry heard a roar like a lion's, and knew it was the gray, realizing that he was heading into a trap.

Once the mustangs were sandwiched between the brush-covered log fences that made the funnel, the cowboys steered their mounts closer to the fences, trying to haze and hurrah the wild horses to keep them moving and to discourage them from trying to break through. Suddenly the big gray, at the head of the herd, stopped and shrilled and reared, trying to turn away from the narrowing gorge. But by now the other mustangs were seized by panic and wouldn't be turned. The leader bellowed with rage, a sound Colbry clearly heard over the tumult, and then he saw the gray shooting down one of the brush-covered fence lines, slamming into a couple of the other mustangs, knocking one of them down, and then leaping like a gazelle over a fence when confronted by a lasso-twirling cowboy. Colbry caught a glimpse of him as he soared over the fence and raced up a slope and into some trees.

The cowboys let him go. They all wanted to try him, but none were foolish enough to think they could take him by their lonesome. The mustang herd thundered into the corral, the entrance was blocked with two logs, and the deal was done. The trapped mustangs whinnied and snorted and reared and slammed into one another, seeking the exit that did not exist. The Rocking Chair cowboys gathered in the funnel, admiring their handiwork and looking at Colbry with newfound respect, since his plan had worked to perfection.

"No rest for the weary, boys," he said, then instructed a couple of the hands to help him remove the brush from the fences that formed the funnel, while dispatching the rest to build third fence across the ravine, using timber that had already been cut, creating a triangular corral attached to the one that held the wild horses. This was done before noon, and by then the mustangs had calmed down. Then the poles keeping the horses in the gulch were removed, and the horses roamed into the triangle. Colbry spent a good bit of time watching them, judging their worth. Once they were spread out it was easy enough to pick the twelve mares they would keep, and he picked seven more besides. After that it was just a matter of riding into them and separating those horses from the rest, coaxing them back into the gulch and letting the rest move into the funnel. It was a long and often frustrating operation, and by the end of it the dust-caked men were tired and thirsty, slumped in their saddles as the sun set. Then the unchosen mustangs were released from the funnel and thundered away. From off in the distance came the bellowing call of the elusive gray, and in no time the other wild ones had vanished, rejoining their leader.

The Rocking Chair men returned to the ranch house and the next few days were spent breaking the nineteen mustangs. It was an arduous and dangerous task. The wild horses were lassoed one at a time by four cowboys, who tried to hold the animal in place long enough for a fifth man to approach, grunting "horse talk" and waving a blanket. The mustang would kick and jump and snort for a while, but eventually stopped its antics and watched the man with the blanket, slowly becoming aware that the humans meant him no real harm. Only then was the halter applied, rawhide straps around the animal's muzzle and behind its ears, and once it was in place, the other cowboys removed their lassos and backed away. That day, one cowboy broke his ankle. Colbry did his share, and was thrown several times. By the end of day he was as sore head to toe as he had ever been, but hadn't broken anything.

Laurie Ruston spent much of the day at the breaking pen, watching the horses intently. She usually stood with Colbry, and her astute observations about this horse or the other impressed him. She knew as much or more than he did about horses, how they were built, how they thought and how they would react in this or that situation, and in the latter case was never wrong. They were both present when Trace Simmons, furious after being thrown by a feisty blue moon mare, picked himself up, dusted himself off, waited until the unruly horse had been lassoed by a couple of cowboys, then walked up to the horse and punched it in the head, hard enough to make the animal stagger.

Before Colbry could react, Laurie had climbed over the fence and marched over to Simmons, who was cursing at the cowboys with the ropes to hold the horse, which was fiddle-footing, snorting and pulling on the ropes, eyes wide with terror. The cowboys managed to hold on, pulling hard to keep the mare from rearing, and themselves being pulled across the corral. Colbry stiffly clambered over the fence and went after Laurie. Simmons saw her coming and turned to face her, scowling. The scowl turned into surprise, and then rage, as Laurie walked right up to him and slapped him hard. Simmons was shocked, and then touched his cheek and his expression became ugly and dangerous. But then his eyes flicked past her to settle on Colbry, who had come up right beside her.

Something in Colbry's expression made Simmons reach for his holster…belatedly becoming aware that no one wore his lead-slinger when breaking horses.

"You're fired," snapped Laurie. "Be off my land by sundown."

Simmons was shocked, and then the shock turned into anger. "Damn mare needed to be shown who's boss or she might kill a man someday," he grumbled.

"And now she's more dangerous than ever, thanks to you!" replied Laurie. "Now get your belongings and come by the house for your pay." With that she turned and left the corral.

Simmons shifted his dark glower to Colbry, who was standing there, watching him, his eyes as cold as blue ice.

"What are you looking at?" growled the former foreman.

"A man who's been taking advantage of Miss Ruston's good nature. And that's over now."

Simmons looked around at the other cowboys, all of whom were quietly and grimly watching the confrontation. He saw no sympathy or support, so looked back at Colbry and sneered, "You haven't seen the last of me, mister."

Colbry nodded. "Well, if I do see you again, I guarantee you it will be the last time."

Simmons snorted, but a glimmer of fear could be seen in his eyes now. He turned away and stalked out of the corral. Colbry waited until the man had disappeared into the bunkhouse, then left the breaking pen and strolled over to the big house. He was on the porch, leaning with arms folded against an upright, when Simmons emerged, saddled his horse, led the mount over to the big house, hitched the cayuse and glowered at Colbry. Then Simmons blinked and looked away, because Colbry's unflinching ice blue gaze was locked onto him. He stepped up onto the porch and as soon as he did, Laurie emerged from the house and handed him some greenbacks. Simmons didn't count the money. Instead, he shoved it in a pocket and without a word climbed aboard his cayuse and rode away. Laurie breathed an audible sigh of relief, then glanced at Colbry.

"We need to talk. Come inside."

She went back into the house and Colbry followed her into the spacious main room. In the center was a fireplace unlike any he had seen before. It was big, open on all sides, with an iron cast flue that funneled the smoke up through the ceiling. A sofa and chairs encircled it. Along the back wall were glass-fronted bookcases. A large oak desk stood in a corner near them. Animal-skin rugs were strategically placed here and there. A couple of framed paintings of rural scenes adorned the walls along with an array of horns, including those of a longhorn steer. Laurie moved to a sideboard and gestured at several bottles and a couple of glasses on a pewter tray, but Colbry shook his head. She poured herself two fingers of brandy into a glass then steered him to the chairs around the fireplace. He waited until she sat in one of them, and, when she gestured for him to do so, sat in one that he turned slightly to face her.

"Well, now I'm short one foreman," she said, sipped from her glass, then added, "Any ideas on who I should pick to replace Simmons?"

Colbry didn't hesitate. "Burr Welken. Best man I've ever known."

"So you aren't interested in the job." She sounded disappointed.

"Well, I…"

Colbry thought it over. He couldn't deny that he liked and admired Laurie Ruston. Nor could he deny that he was attracted to the brown-haired beauty. He had seen some pretty whores, but none as fetching as Laurie. But he knew he wasn't in her league, and that she could do much better. Not that she had ever shown that kind of interest in him. She had always been a lady in his presence. So it wasn't that he feared a more intimate relationship with her. He just wondered if he could be dependable enough. In that moment he realized he had never been true to anything really, not for very long, and for once in his life he was more concerned about someone else than he was about his own wants and desires.

"It's just that I'm not sure how long…"

Laurie smiled pensively, and nodded. She put a finger to her lips. "Shh. I trust you. And I need you." Realizing how that sounded as soon as the words passed her lips, she blushed. "I mean, I need you to help me. I need a man I know I can trust." She studied his expression for a moment, head tilted slightly to one side. "For as long as you can."

Colbry drew a long breath and let it out slowly. Then he nodded. "Okay, I'll do it. For a while anyway. See how it suits me."

"If you left any belongings at the line cabin…"

"I didn't. What you see is everything I own."

"Your predecessor stayed in a spare room here at the house. To be honest, I don't know why my father allowed it." She fell silent, and Colbry read the profound grief in her expression and posture as she thought about John Ruston. Then she managed to put aside her grief and smile. "You're welcome to…"

He shook his head. "No, that won't do. The bunkhouse will suit me."

She nodded. "Yes, I suppose that would be best. Shall I summon the men and tell them about your promotion?"

Colbry declined the offer with a shake of his head, even though he was aware that many of the Rocking Chair hands didn't know much, if anything, about him since he had spent most of his time on the ranch payroll as a line rider. There was a possibility that a few of them might resent his promotion, men who had been riding for the brand longer than he had. "I'll handle that."

"Well, if any of them don't believe you, send them to me."

He smiled, realizing that what she suggested was the last thing he could do. If a man challenged his authority he couldn't afford to go running to the boss to ask her to handle the situation. "I won't need to, but thanks."

Returning to the breaking pen, he spent the rest of the day working with the other hands, doing his share of bronco-busting. He ate supper with the others in the bunkhouse, dining on an inch-thick steak and potatoes, courtesy of Alonso. When he was finished eating, he waited for a break in the conversation.

"A few of you may not know me yet. The name is Colbry. Used to ride the line. But now Trace Simmons is gone, and I'm the new foreman."

The cowboys looked at each other, and then some of them shrugged and all went back to eating. Most of them identified themselves. Colbry didn't detect even a glimmer of resentment. After all had eaten their fill, some of them headed outside to sit on the bunkhouse porch, talking and smoking some before bed while watching the night deepen. A few others went to their bunks, and a couple sat at the table drinking coffee with Colbry, who mentioned that, unlike Simmons, he intended to bunk here with the rest of them. A cowboy named Luke pointed out an unclaimed bunk and Colbry wasted no time stretching his aching body out on it. Luke lingered a moment.

"For one, I can't say I'm sorry to see Trace is gone. He always thought he was better than us."

"He wasn't," replied Colbry. "And I'm not, either."

Pleased, Luke nodded and smiled, then went outside to join his compadres on the porch.

Colbry usually fell asleep as soon as he put his head down, but that night he was restless. He realized that accepting Laurie's offer of the foreman's job meant he had committed to staying in one place for a good long while, and that ran counter to his lifelong habit of rambling when the urge struck him. He had remained in the employ of the Rocking Chair ranch for almost two years while John Ruston had lived because as a line rider he was pretty much on his own. Perhaps he shouldn't have taken the job of foreman, but for some reason he had a difficult time turning Laurie down. He wondered why that was the case. The only answer he could come up with made him uncomfortable because it was obvious. There was no way around it. He liked Laurie Ruston to a degree that unsettled him. Had that been the reason he had turned down the offer of a room in the big house?

There was nothing like a woman to make a man think about putting down roots. Something he had never done in his entire life.

Chapter Nine

Barrett Faulkner was idling away his day toying with one of his female Mexican house servants when a pair of riders came up the long, oak-shaded road to reach the Elmwood plantation house. He kept several of such women in the Greek Revival mansion he had built almost two decades earlier, finding them much preferable to his young southern belle wife, several years dead now from a broken neck after falling down the spiral staircase in the marble-floored grand hall of the main house. Blanche had been a spoiled, self-obsessed woman who had often balked at the prospect of congress with her husband, especially after learning how rough he could be. The servant girls, on the other hand, had no right to complain about anything. He had picked them up in San Antonio and he paid them well.

The house itself was unusual for the bush country of west-central Texas, where most were built of adobe and timber. Having seen the adobe and stone fortress that had been the residence of his neighbor John Ruston, he had decided to out-do the Rocking Chair owner and build a home reminiscent of the one in which had been his birthplace back in Louisiana. He thought his manor much more stately and attractive than John Ruston's little fort.

When he heard the cantering horses approaching, he pushed the servant girl off his lap without so much as a by-your-leave and strolled to the open double doors across the room, which served as his library, the walls covered with book shelves laden with bound books he had never bothered to read. He had designed the home himself, with the help of a talented architect he had imported from Baltimore, and the double doors were in lieu of the tall windows normally found in Greek Revival homes. The library itself was meant solely to impress guests. He thought the library left others with the impression that he was a very educated man, which was in fact far from the truth.

Faulkner paused just inside the room, to study the riders through the gossamer curtains that danced slowly in the summer breeze. He was a tall, slender man, with a paunch that his highly skilled tailor could not entirely obscure. His brown hair had turned mostly white, and was brushed straight back from his face, and long enough in the back to dangle over the high collar of his shirt. He opened a thermidor, removed a cigar, and lighted it with a safety match, all the while eying the men as they checked their mounts at the front steps. A male servant appeared to take charge of the horses. Once he recognized the arrivals, Faulkner stepped out onto the wide, columned porch that completely circled the house, with eight columns, twelve-feet apart, across the front and back and six columns on each side.

The two men saw him and approached with long, urgent strides. Faulkner knew one of them quite well. It was his son and only heir, Merle, a slender, bearded young man. The other was built like a lumberjack, yellow-haired, and clad in buckskins. He walked with a hitch in his stride and stood with a slouch. Faulkner didn't know him or most of his hands by name, since he left the day-to-day operations of the ranch to Merle. Both men were armed with side guns, and both of them swept their hats off their heads as soon as they'd seen him and didn't get too close, stopping about six feet away, a respectful distance.

"Rory and me were jawing after breakfast this morning about those Rocking Chair beeves we made off with," said Merle. "He has an idea I thought you'd like to hear."

Faulkner was scowling. "Rory and I," he muttered. He liked to maintain the pretense that he was an educated man and use of the proper pronoun was one of the few things he knew. He gestured for the two men to follow and went back inside. When she saw that he had company with him, the Mexican house servant he had been toying with earlier, and who now stood meekly beside the chair in which he had been sitting, hurried out of the room, trying to mask her vast relief. Faulkner returned to the chair and sat down, leaning his head back and puffing on his cigar, gesturing at the round side table near at hand, on which rested a tray with a bottle of brandy and several shot glasses. "Help yourself, Rory," he said, "then do tell me this idea of yours."

Merle poured two shot glasses with the brandy while Rory, ringing the hat in his hands, murmured, "Well, sir, I know where you could sell a whole lot of stolen livestock, much more than we took from the Rocking Chair that last time."

"Do you now. How long have you worked for me, Rory?"

"Coming up on three winters, sir."

"Go on."

"Well, before I came here I worked down around the Mexican border, and so I heard about a Comanchero town down thataways. It was said there were at least a hundred of them, maybe more. They trade with the Apaches and Comanches."

"Trade what?"

"Anything them Injuns could steal. Cattle, sheep, women."

"In exchange for what?"

"Horses, gold and silver. See, the Injuns mostly raided south. They hit rancheros and mines and small towns."

Faulkner pondered a moment, and a crooked smile curled his mouth. "Must be pure hell for honest men down there."

"Point is," said Merle, "You can steal a lot more Ruston cattle, push 'em down south, sell 'em all direct to the Comancheros. Beats taking a handful of unbranded cows now and then and putting your own mark on them. Before long, that Ruston woman won't be able to hold onto her ranch, and you'll be all the richer for it."

Faulkner puffed on his cigar some more and said nothing for several minutes as he considered the suggestion. He was silent for so long that Rory glanced at Merle and hiked his eyebrows, accompanied by a querulous shrug of his shoulders.

"We'll need more hands for that," Faulkner said, finally. "Ten more at least if we're going to do it."

"So, are we?" asked Merle. "Gonna do it, I mean."

A slow grin wrinkled Faulkner's gaunt cheeks. "Why not? I want both of you to ride to San Antone and pick up some men. Men who are skilled with both livestock and firearms and who don't care what side of the law they stand on. But don't tarry there too long."

Merle finished off his drink, nodded, then took the empty shot glass from his companion, placed it on the tray, and led Rory outside. But at the doorway he told Rory to go on, then returned to his father, helped himself to another shot of brandy, then tilted his head curiously as he stared at Faulkner.

"Pa, you've never told me why you hate the Rustons so much."

"It's none of your business."

"The hell it isn't," snapped Merle. "I can maybe understand why you hated John Ruston. He was your rival. You two had been butting heads my whole life about one thing or another, even though there's more than enough land and cattle and horses to go around. But you both wanted to be the top dog in these parts. Thing is, Laurie Ruston has never done anything to you. She hasn't even been in Texas for years. But you want to run her off, or destroy her. I will stand with you no matter what you do, but I think I deserve to know why."

Faulkner stood up quickly, anger twisting his features, but Merle didn't back down, despite being all too aware of his father's quick and sometimes violent temper. Faulker relaxed as quickly as he had bristled. He began to pace, hands clasped behind his back, staring down at the rug beneath his booted feet. In the silence, Merle heard the flies that had gotten through the curtains on the open door to the porch and that were now buzzing lazily high up near the raised ceiling.

"Fine," said Faulkner, turning suddenly to face his son. "I will never forgive John Ruston because he...he was intimate with my wife. Your mother! He was in between wives of his own at the time." He was sneering now. "And he had a child with her, a child named Laurie."

Merle's eyes widened and his jaw dropped. "You mean...Laurie Ruston is my half-sister?"

Faulkner stepped closer and jabbed a finger into his son's chest. "Laurie Ruston is your enemy and don't you forget it! Now get to work. I want you and Rory to ride for San Antone at first light and be back the next day with men who know their way around cattle. And remember, they have gun hands, too."

"Yeah. I know that, Pa," said Merle, sarcastically.

"Don't take that tone with me, boy! All this, all that I've built, will be yours soon enough. Don't get in a hurry for me to end up six feet under."

Merle and Rory had just turned and started walking away from the big house, while Faulkner had just settled in his chair, when a rider came down the oak-shaded road. Faulkner stood up and went to the open door. When the rider stopped in front of Merle and Rory, Faulkner could see him well enough to know he wasn't an Elmwood employee. He had never seen the rider before. Merles grabbed the horse's bridle, since the horse was fiddle-footing as horses were wont to do after a long run, and the two men spoke for a while. Merle looked over his shoulder in his father's direction, then spoke to the man, and then to Rory. Rory walked away while the horseman dismounted and accompanied Merle back to the house.

"This feller claims he used to work on the Rocking Chair spread," Merle said. "Says his name is…"

"My name is Trace Simmons," said the other, and t hen said no more, watching Faulkner in the way of a man who expected his name to trigger a reaction.

"I've heard of you," said Faulkner. "You're the foreman of the Rocking Chair."

Simmons grimaced. "Not no more I ain't. Laurie Ruston fired me. So I come here looking for twork."

"Hmm." Faulkner's head tilted slightly as he looked the man over. "And why did she send you packing?"

"She said 'cause she didn't like the way I was handling one of the mustangs a crew brought in. But if you ask me, there's more to it than that. You see, there's a man by the name of Cord Colbry."

"I don't think I know him."

"Probably not. He's been a linerider. Rode the western property line for a couple years. Then John Ruston put him in charge of the herd that was pushed on up to Ellsworth in the spring. That's where he met Miss Ruston. And when they got back to the Rocking Chair she fired me and gave Colbry my job." He growled the last sentence with plenty of venom.

Faulkner glanced at Merle, who shrugged, indicating he had no worthwhile information about what Simmons had just claimed.

"I'm curious. Why didn't you push that herd to market, Mr. Simmons?"

"I had to stay put on account of the rustlin' problem we've been having."

"Well, I have a foreman," said Faulkner, and nodded in Merle's direction. "My son, Merle, fills those boots."

Simmons shrugged his massive shoulders. "Fine with me. I'm just looking for a job. Been cowboying all my life, Mr. Faulkner. I don't think there's much if anything I can't do."

Faulkner pursed his lips, studying Simmons, then made up his mind. The fact that Simmons seemed to hold a grudge against Laurie Ruston was a positive, in his view. "Okay. Thirty dollars a month and board." He paused, then decided to test the newcomer and watched him keenly as he remarked, "And you might be interested in knowing that Merle is going to San Antonio to sign up more men. You see, I've decided to wage war on Miss Ruston and the Rocking Chair ranch"

Simmons' eyes lit up and a cold, half-smile curled the corners of his mouth. "Sounds to me like I've come to the right place, then."

Faulkner smiled and nodded. "With these extra hands, I intend to make off with as many Rocking Chair cattle as we can round up and push them down to the border where they will be sold."

Simmons' smile turned into a broad grin. "I hope I can be a part of that, Mr. Faulkner."

"Maybe you will be. Merle, show him around and get him settled in." He looked back at Simmons. "You can ride with my son to San Antonio tomorrow."

When Luther Keyes arrived in Lampasas, in the company of his sister and the three longriders he'd had the great misfortune of running into back in the Indian Territories, he began to do what he did best: gambling. There were several saloons in town, and he moved from one to another. He didn't cheat, though he was handy at it, because he didn't need to in order to win and didn't want to take any chances. While he played, Mary Keyes usually sat beside him, serving as a distraction to the other players. Meanwhile Joe, Frank and Monte – the hardcases he had cut a deal with back in the Territories – roamed the town and watched the main street, often lounging in front of the watering holes and keeping an eye out for horses marked with the Rocking Chair brand while downing prodigious quantities of beer and whiskey.

Keyes was aware that there was a chance he might run into Clay Colbry. But based on his past experiences with the man, he didn't take Colbry for a cold-blooded killer who would shoot him on sight. If they did run into one another, he had come up with an explanation: that Sheriff Whitman had run him out of town after the events in Ellsworth, and since he was already persona non grata in Abilene and had no prospects apart from being murdered and maybe even scalped in the Territories, had ventured into Texas and then had just happened to find himself in Lampasas, which had already earned a name for itself as an up and coming frontier town. He was aware that there were holes in the story, one being that a gambler would likely find the grass greener in a bigger pasture, like San Antonio. He could counter with a story that no one could argue with: that the competition in San Antonio would be great, and so the grass seemed a lot greener in Lampasas.

It wasn't long before Keyes had a Rocking Chair cowboy at his table. He knew it would happen sooner or later; Lampasas was the only town where cowboys working for that brand could come to for whiskey and women. Only then did Keyes begin to cheat, and he did it to favor of the cowboy, who wasn't very good at poker. Even so, he won a fair number of hands, and Keyes would toss more money into the pot than he ordinarily would, and occasionally even broke a good hand with a discard, just to keep the cowboy, whose name was Josh Street, in the game. Mary did her share, casually flirting with the other men at the table, and paying Street a little more attention than the rest.

After nearly an hour of play, and once Street had a nice pile of money in front of him, Keyes dealt the cowboy three aces and began betting heavily. The other two players folded early on but the Rocking Chair cowboy stayed in. He had been drinking a good deal, so much so that Keyes had offered to buy him a couple of drinks. It was better than seeing the pots get smaller as a result. Keyes didn't call until almost all of Street's money was in the middle of the table. He didn't wonder that the cowboy had thought he'd won the hand. As was usually the case in frontier poker, the deck consisted of only twenty cards, the face cards and four tens and the only hand that could beat him were four of a kind.

Then Keyes called. Street grinned ear-to-ear and exclaimed "I got you whupped!" loud enough to turn heads as he showed his hand. Keyes smiled politely and showed his hand. He had four jacks, having dealt two of them from the bottom of the deck, where he had placed them in the shuffle. It was the oldest trick in the book, and he had mastered it early on in his career.

The cowboy's jaw literally dropped and he stared blankly at the cards.

"You had a very good hand," said Keyes humbly. "I just got lucky. Finally."

Street's shocked expression suddenly turned ugly. He abruptly got to his feet, and in so doing knocked his chair backward. Nearly every head in the saloon turned, and the din of a multitude of voices suddenly diminished drastically. The cowboy's hand dropped to the grip of the six-shooter in his holster but before he could get the gun halfway out of the leather Mary Keyes brought the .41 caliber Remington over-and-under out of her reticule. She was quite calm. It wasn't the first time that a loser at the table had threatened her brother. In fact it happened a number of times, because not only was Luther Keyes a better-than-average player, he was a very skilled card sharp. A large majority of the men who sat down to play cards with her brother lost money, and some lost a lot of money.

A shocked expression on Street's face melted into one of fear and he very slowly took his trembling hand off the butt of his pistola. Seconds later a burly man came up and grabbed Street's arm with one hand and pushed him roughly against the wall behind him, hard enough that it bounced the back of Street's skull off the wall and stunned him. It was the man Keyes had figured out was a lawman shortly after he had sat down to play poker. The burly man was well-dressed compared to most of the denizens. He had gotten a drink at the bar and hadn't had to pay for it. And eventually, when he turned around and braced his elbows on the bar, Keyes had spotted the badge under his unbuttoned coat, pinned to his vest.

The lawman glanced at the derringer in Mary's hand and said, gruffly. "You can put that away, miss." It obviously was not a suggestion, but a demand. Mary smiled demurely and obeyed.

"I am so sorry," she said, convincingly contrite. "I was very much afraid that he was going to shoot my brother."

The other two players at the table quickly gathered up what was left of their money, then got up, intent on getting as far away from the table as they could.

The lawman looked at Luther Keyes with cold, emotionless eyes. Keyes smiled politely and pushed a generous portion of the money in the pot across the table toward Street.

"I don't want him to walk away stone-broke," he explained.

The lawman appropriated Street's pistol. "Keep it," growled the lawman. "Name's Ben Mackey. That's Sheriff Ben Mackey to you. Been watching you, mister. You're a card sharp."

"I make a living with cards and am usually on good terms with Lady Luck. I have acquired a certain aptitude for the work. But I don't cheat. You are welcome to search me. No cards up my sleeve."

Mackey shook his head. "Nah, you're too handy with those cards for that. I reckon if you cheat you do it with sleight of hand, but I watched you for a while and damn it, I couldn't tell for sure."

Keyes's pleasant expression didn't change a bit. His smile remained warm. "You could watch me until hell froze over and you wouldn't see me cheat. What will happen to this cowboy?"

"He's going to spend a night or two in jail. Will let him sober up. He rides for the Rocking Chair brand and he has some compadres in town, so I'll make sure they take the word back home that he's in the hoosegow. Someone will have to come bail him out. I don't generally provide a man food and shelter without collecting bail money. Of course it goes into the town coffers."

"Of course it does." Keyes took off his hat and scooped his winnings into it, then rose. "I think my sister and I are done here, Sheriff."

Mackey smiled a crooked smile. "I think you're right. You're done in this saloon. If you want to deal somewhere else, try the saloon over on the Mex side of town. Take their pesos for all I care. And stay out of trouble. I have a cell waiting for you if this kind of horseshit happens again."

It took Keyes a moment to stuff the greenbacks and the hard money into his various pockets. He left a generous gratuity on the bar in front of the barkeep and then he and Mary went outside. Across the street, Joe was sprawled in a chair in front of a general store. His two partners were sitting to the left and right of him. Luther and Mary made their way across the wide, hardpack street. Mary was keenly uneasy approaching the men who would have raped her back in the Territories, and possibly murdered her, had her brother not come up with a scheme that appealed to these cutthroats even more. While grateful to her brother for his quick wits, she couldn't get past the feeling that they couldn't be trusted, and a fear lingered in her mind. It had kept her awake most of the night for at least a week.

"I guess you saw the sheriff haul a man off to jail," Keyes told the trio of hardcases. "That cowboy rides for the Rocking Chair ranch. Word of it will get back to Laurie Ruston before long."

"What makes you think she'll come herself to bail him out?" asked Joe, skeptically.

"It'll be her or Clay Colbry, most likely." Luther Keyes paused as a man stepped out of the general store, sacks of seed under both arms. The man walked to his wagon, which was pulled up in front of the dentist's office next door since there was no room to spare in front of the general store. Keyes waited until the man had loaded the sacks in the wagon bed, climbed up onto the bench and whipped his two-mule team into motion. "And if it's Colbry, feel free to kill him. He's a fair gun-hand, but I'm guessing you don't mind bushwhacking a man. And that will bring Laurie Ruston here for sure."

Joe looked at his companions, then fastened his cold, dark eyes on Luther Keyes. "It better. 'Cause if it doesn't, you'll pay." He glanced past Luther at Mary and a grin creased his cheeks, a grin that chilled Mary to the bone. "And me and my boys will finish what we started with your sister."

Chapter Ten

When the Rocking Chair cowboy reached the ranch house, Clay Colbry was standing alongside Laurie at the breaking pen. The last few mustangs they had brought in were being broken. Laurie wanted to oversee the process because she couldn't abide seeing any horse mistreated. Colbry was there more out of concern for the cowboys, since he was now responsible for them. And he couldn't deny to himself that he liked spending time with Laurie Ruston.

The cowboy who had ridden hell-for-leather from Lampasas had boots on the ground before his cayuse had come to a complete stop He swept the hat off his head and slapped it against his chaps-covered legs to disperse the dust. Something about his haste and his expression caused a furrow to appear on Laurie's forehead, and she went to him immediately, with Colbry tagging along, since it was clear by the cowboy's arrival and the expression on his face that something was amiss.

"Hadley Street's been locked up," he blurted.

"For what reason?" asked Laurie.

"He was playing poker at the Buckhorn. I was at the bar, halfway watching, because he was playing with a man who looked stem to stern like a gambler. Sure 'nuff, it didn't take long before Hadley had lost all his pay. He was a little drunk, I guess, because he jumped up and looked like he was about to pull his smoke-maker, but the gambler beat him to the draw. No one fired a shot 'cause Sheriff Mackey happened to be there and stepped in. He took Street to jail. And, knowing Mackey, he'll stay locked up until someone shows up to pay for him to get out."

It was clear as day that Laurie was angry. "Take care of your horse. And saddle Beholden," she said, curtly, then spun around and walked with quick strides into the house.

"Damn law-dog," muttered the cowboy. "He's the type who'll lock you up if he don't like the way you spit on the street. Makes good money at it, too." He glanced at Colbry, then led his horse to the stable.

Colbry followed him, and while the cowboy was saddling Beholden, he had Boots rigged out and was walking back to the ranch house, leading the buckskin. When he got there, Laurie was waiting impatiently on the front porch, loading her 1873 Winchester.

"Expecting trouble?" asked Colbry.

She pulled a wad of greenbacks out of a pocket of her riding skirt and offered it to Colbry. "Since apparently you are coming along, you can take care of this. Should be enough to get Street and myself out of jail."

"What makes you think you might end up behind bars?"

"I've never met him. Mackey, I mean. But something tells me he and I won't get along."

Colbry took the money and put it in his saddlebags. When Beholden arrived and she was in the saddle, he mounted up.

"I'm glad you're coming," she remarked and heeled her thoroughbred into a canter.

When they arrived in Lampasas it was getting late, with about an hour of daylight left. As was his habit when entering a town, Colbry put eyes on every person he could see. He spotted three men lounging on benches in front of a dentistry across the street. One of them was puffing away at a cheroot, and a pale cloud of smoke moved in languorous wreaths over his head. There were plenty of men who sat in the shade of the boardwalks and whiled away their time watching the comings and goings on a busy street. But something about these men made him look longer than usual. They weren't talking to each other. They weren't just passing the time of day. They were obviously watching the sheriff's office, while passing a bottle of who-hit-john between themselves. One of them was smoking a cheroot. Colbry sensed they were waiting for something… or someone. So after dismounting and tying Boots to the hitching post, he drew the 50-70 Sharps out of its saddle boot and carried it into the sheriff's office, following in Laurie's wake.

Sheriff Mackey was sitting behind his desk, booted feet propped up on his kneehole desk, the local newspaper in hand. He looked up at the pair who entered and his bushy brows furrowed, since he didn't recognize either one of them. But when Laurie identified herself, he grinned, got his feet down, tossed the newspaper on his cluttered desk and pushed himself out of his chair, picking up a ring of keys off his cluttered desktop.

"I reckon you've come to get your man out," he said.

"What are the charges?" asked Laurie.

Mackey rubbed his chin, thinking for a moment. "I oughta say attempted suicide. He had lost his poke to, and was about to draw on, a gambler in the Last Chance. I did your hotheaded hand a favor."

"There's a law in this town against suicide?" drawled Colbry. He had stopped just inside the door and taken one step to the right, so he could half-turn his head and see the street. through the room's sole window. At the same time, he was further to the sheriff's left, which meant that if for some reason the lawman pulled iron he would have to swing it across his body to aim it at Colbry, which gave the latter an extra second, all he would need. It wasn't that Colbry expected Mackey to use his shooting iron. It was just a deeply ingrained habit to pick the best spot in the event that violence erupted.

Mackey gave him an ugly look. "I saved his life, mister. A jail cell was the best place for him to cool his heels. And the safest place, too."

"When were you planning to set him free?" asked Laurie.

"The policy is that he stays overnight. But you can get him out early and take him home. Either way, you pay for his room and board. And a small extra fee if you want to take him now."

Laurie glanced over her shoulder at Colbry, who shrugged. He didn't see any way around it. In all his travels he had never run into a local lawman who extorted money for a prisoner's release, at least not north of the border. The only recourse he could think of was to force Mackey to release Street, but an outlaw's life was the one thing he hadn't experienced and didn't want to.

"How much?" asked Laurie, an icy tone to her voice.

Mackey grinned and rubbed his chin. "Well, let's see. Ten dollars ought to do it."

Laurie was wearing a small coin purse attached to the leather belt round her slim waist, and from this she took two gold half-eagles from it and dropped them in the town sheriff's palm. Mackey disappeared through a door into the jail block. He returned a moment later with Street, who glanced at Laurie. shame-faced, and then at Colbry.

"Where's his horse?" asked Colbry.

Mackey shrugged. "Maybe still out on the street. If it isn't there, let me know."

"I shudder to think how much it would cost to get you to do your job and track a horse thief," remarked Laurie.

The sheriff glowered at her, and then at Colbry, who barked a laugh at Laurie's caustic comment.

Once outside, Street found his horse, with Laurie and Colbry following him, leading their own mounts by rein leather. Once they were all in their saddles, the sheepish cowboy spoke.

"I'm real sorry, Miss Ruston. "That card sharp got my goat. I'd swear on my mother's grave that he was cheating."

"Then you should have checked out of the game," said Colbry. "If you'd shot him dead you would have swung for it."

"It's over and done," said Laurie. She clearly didn't want to discuss the matter. "Lets' go home."

Colbry kept sweeping the street with his steely gaze as they rode out of Lampasas, with Laurie between them. He held the rein leather in his left hand, with his right resting on the stock of the Sharps rifle that was back in its scabbard. The men he had noticed earlier, the ones who had been watching the sheriff's office, didn't move. Once they were out of town, Colbry drew a deep breath and took his hand off the 50-70. But he didn't stop glancing over his shoulder to check their back trail.

They were bushwhacked less than an hour later, crossing open country in the growing dusk when a gunshot rang out. The bullet hit Street's mount before the sound reached them. To his credit Street landed on his feet as his horse went down with a shrill whinny. The animal thrashed, struggling to get to its feet, but Colbry knew in a glance it wasn't going to ever get up again. It lay that grunting and shrilling. Shouting Street's name, Colbry turned Boots sharply, extending an arm. Street's first instinct was to take cover behind the fallen horse. Instead he grabbed Colbry's arm and swung his lithe frame up behind the buckskin's rider. Colbry drew his Schofield pistol and put the fallen horse out of its misery, then shouted "Ride!" to Laurie and kicked Boots into a leaping gallop. Scanning the tree line, he saw several muzzle flashes and heard the buzzing whine of bullets in the air.

Colbry knew that there was a ravine just a few hundred yards away. Once in it he checked Boots sharply. Laurie was right behind him, and did likewise with Beholden. Street dismounted before Boots had come to a complete stop, crawled up one side of the ravine and began returning fire. The shooters had moved further west in the trees and were still shooting. Sliding out of the saddle, Colbry threw an arm over Boot's neck while pulling down on the reins, which brought the buckskin's head down. Changing his stance, he put all his weight onto the animal's neck, telling the horse "Down … down" in Apache. Boots lay down. A quick look over his shoulder revealed that Laurie was doing the same thing, and Beholden complied gracefully.

"Stay down!" Colbry yelled to Laurie and then got up, only to drag the Sharps rifle out of its boot and, kneeling on his buckskin's neck to discourage the horse from trying to rise, got off several shots, rapid-fire, into the trees where the muzzle flash was located. Street was shooting too.

The hostile fire ceased and Colbry dropped down across his horse's neck again.

"Are you two okay?" asked Laurie.

She seemed quite calm, and Colbry was impressed, especially when he considered it quite possible that she had never been under fire on before.

"Yeah," grunted Street, then glanced at his horse and grumbled, "But I'm madder than a nest full of hornets."

"Think about it later," advised Colbry. "Mad can get you killed."

"Do you think they will give up and go away?"

Colbry shook his head. "No way of knowing." He checked the western skyline, now emblazoned with dusk's first blazing shades of red. "Sun'll be down in ten, fifteen minutes, then they might try to sneak closer. They might fall back and wait until daylight. Or they might go away."

"Who are they?"

"My guess is they're men I saw in Lampasas. Three fellers, rough around the edges, who were keeping an eagle eye on the sheriff's office when we were there. But I could be wrong. Might just be outlaws. Still some of them in these parts."

"Or maybe Comanches?" asked Street.

"I don't think so. Comanches may lay in wait, but once the trap is sprung you'll hear from them. Taunts and curses and such."

"So what do we do?"

Colbry checked the darkening sky. The remnants of sunlight was quickly melting away. He could already see a few stars. It was going to be a clear night, but the moon wouldn't appear for another hour.

"In a few minutes we cut and run. Street, you will get on behind me. If they start shooting again you shoot back."

He tossed the Sharps to the Rocking Chair cowboy. "There are extra cartridges in my saddlebags." He looked at Laurie. "Can he get up and go?"

Laurie knew he meant Boots, and she nodded. "You can count on it."

Colbry told Street to fire a couple more rounds into the trees, but the shots garnered no response.

"Maybe we ran 'em off?" asked the Rocking Chair hand.

"Maybe. Or they're waiting until the sun goes down to sneak in closer."

Street looked over his shoulder at Colbry. "But we won't be here?"

Colbry shook his head.

"I reckon we can't carry my saddle."

"No. But we'll come back for it."

When the last streaks of sunset abandoned the sky and stars began to show, it was dark enough to make spotting a target from more than a hundred yards unlikely, and Colbry let Boots up and gave Street a hand up behind him. Laurie was already in the saddle and they wasted no time riding further down the ravine a hundred yards and then broke cover and rode hell-for-leather westward. A couple of gunshots sounded in the distance but then the range was too late. Street kept an eye out behind them but in a few minutes he said. "I don't see or hear 'em!"

Just to be sure, Colbry suddenly steered Boots northward and over a low swell of open ground, then reined in the buckskin. Laurie followed suit, and they waited in the gathering gloom for a spell. Colbry dismounted and put his ear to the ground for a moment, then stood up and said "No one's following." He climbed aboard Boots and helped Street up behind him again, then steered his buckskin with unerring accuracy in the direction of the Rocking Chair buildings, keeping the north star, which always led the other stars into the night sky, over his right shoulder.

The next morning at dawn Colbry was in front of the barn, saddling Boots, when Laurie showed up, rubbing the sleep out of her eyes. The birds in the tall elm tree that provided partial shade for two of the corrals were also waking up, and singing to each other. The wild horses they had recently collected were restless, circling the pole fence that restrained them; a young stallion was nipping at the thighs of a few mares, which just annoyed the latter and made them snort and whinny and raise up a cloud of dust that drifted Colbry's way.

"You're up early," she remarked, with a gentle smile.

"You are, too."

She shrugged and looked down. "I have to say, it rattled me. The ambush."

"That's nothing to be ashamed of. Rattled me, too."

She was at the head of his buckskin, and Boots whickered his pleasure as she stroked his head from forelock to muzzle. "Who do you think did it?"

"That's what I'm going to find out."

All the drowsy aftereffects of a long, deep sleep vanished from Laurie's face. "What are you thinking of doing?"

"Going to pick up the trail of whoever was shooting at us and see where it leads."

Looking worried, Laurie thought about it, and in the meantime, Colbry climbed into the saddle. She stepped around to the side of the buckskin and laid her hand on his leg. "Why do you have to go alone?"

He grinned. "I make a lot less noise when I'm alone. Don't worry about me."

She shrugged. "What if I can't help but worry?"

That caught him by surprise, but he didn't say anything, He didn't know what to say. He touched the brim of his old campaign hat and murmured "Be back soon" and she stepped away from Boots as he turned his horse and rode away at a canter, looking back once to see her still standing there, watching him go.

The morning sun was about two hours high in the eastern sky when Colbry arrived at the spot where he and Laurie and Street had been ambushed. The vultures were already feasting on the carcass of Street's dead horse. From that spot, Colbry turned toward the line of trees where the ambushers had lain in wait, and it didn't take him long to pick up their trail as they headed east by north, heading straight for Lampasas. Several times he checked Boots, dismounted, and studied the hoof marks of the horses the men were riding, and eventually he picked up on one mark slightly different from the rest. The horse had been poorly shod on the left hind leg. One of the horseshoe nails had not been driven straight into the hoof's quarter and the head had been deformed by the hammer and was bent a bit so that it left a small straight line. By a stroke of luck, he also found a half-smoked cheroot on the trail.

It meant his instincts about the three hombres he had seen from the window of the sheriff's office yesterday had been sound. They had been watching the office, the same men who had pulled off the ambush later that day. In all likelihood they had been aware that Sheriff Mackey had jailed a Rocking Chair cowboy and were keeping an eye out for Laurie Ruston. Colbry rode out of the woods and returned to the tracks that he and his two companions had made on their home from Lampasas to the Rocking Chair, and soon confirmed by the tracks that the men who had fired at him, Laurie and Street had followed them out of Lampasas.

But why? He had never seen the trio before yesterday. So he didn't imagine he had been their target. Maybe they had a score to settle with Street. Or maybe they were out to gun down Laurie Ruston. If the latter was the case, they were most likely hired killers, because as far as he knew Laurie hadn't done anything to anybody that would warrant her becoming the target for cold-blooded murder. But maybe she didn't have to do anything. Maybe it was because she had taken over the Rocking Chair. How could he find out if there was anyone who might resent her appearance on the scene to take over running the ranch after John Ruston's death?

Arriving in Lampasas, he held Boots to a slow walk down the street, which was bustling as usual. He had been around long enough to know that John Burleson, a veteran of the Texas Revolution, had received a land grant here in return for his services to the Republic and Burleson had established a little settlement which was initially named after him. But the name was soon changed to Lampasas Springs due to the existence of seven mineral springs in the area. It had been so named by a Spanish expedition a hundred and fifty years earlier because the Spaniards were reminded of Lampazos, a Mexican town that also had a lot of natural springs.

Colbry was looking for the three men who had staked out the sheriff's office the day before, but he didn't see them on the main street and was beginning to think he would have to search for them in the town's saloons, or even its bordello, when he saw one of them entering the Buckhorn Saloon, the same cantina where Street had sat down to the card game that had resulted in his doing jail time.

Tying Boots to a hitching post, Colbry pulled the Sharps rifle from its saddle boot and walked into the Buckhorn, stepping to one side just inside the opened doors to let his eyes adjust from the bright sunshine that had been in his eyes during his journey from the Rocking Chair to the relative gloom of the interior. At this time of day there weren't a lot of people in the saloon: two men at a faro table at which the banker wore a flashy vest and a derby hat, two more at a table near the plate glass window up front that was emblazoned with the name of the establishment, and one, accompanied by a saloon girl, at the long mahogany bar serviced by a single bartender, who was wearing another derby hat. This bartender looked up at Colbry as the latter stepped across the threshold, and noticed the rifle and looked a bit concerned. The man with the saloon girl glanced at Colbry and then away, quickly. After refilling the whiskey glasses in front of the man at the bar, he wandered over and put a smile on his face that almost looked authentic.

"Howdy, mister. Name your poison."

"Mezcal."

The bartender nodded and turned to the backbar to fetch a clean glass and a bottle, placed the former in front of Colbry and filled it from the bottle, talking as he poured. "Always keep a bottle handy in case we get a visit from some vaqueros. You from down the border way?"

"I've been there. Chasing Apaches."

The bartender looked impressed. "What brings you up this way?"

"A job. I ride for the Rocking Chair brand."

"I knew John Ruston. Good man. Haven't met his daughter yet. How do you like working for a woman?"

Colbry knocked back the tequila and looked around. Every man there was glancing at him now. "I don't mind it. Except when someone tries to bushwhack me."

The bartender's expression changed from pleasant to concerned. It wasn't that he was worried about people getting bushwhacked as much as he was worried by the Sharps and Colbry's stone-cold expression. Now Colbry's gaze was fastened on the man who was belly up to the bar about six feet to his left, the one accompanied by the flirty saloon girl, who seemed to have no trouble persuading her mark to buy her – and himself – another glass of who-hit-john.

"Hey, you," said Colbry.

The man glanced past the girl to look at him, and the grin he had been wearing faded away. It was obvious that he knew Colbry. Instead of responding he knocked back another shot and spoke to the girl. "Why don't you and me go upstairs for a little private party?"

"You aren't going upstairs," said Colbry. He had recognized the man as one of the trio who had been watching the jail when he and Laurie had come to town to buy Street's freedom. "You're coming out onto the street with me."

"Why the hell would I want to do that?"

"Because you either show me your horse or face me in a fair fight, in which case I will kill you the same way you tried to kill me and Laurie Ruston yesterday."

"I don't know what you're talking about!" He looked around, perhaps hoping his two bushwhacking partners were in the house, or maybe Mackey. In the meantime, the saloon girl, realizing that she was in the middle of a situation that could get bloody, left the man without a word and went all the way to the back of the Buckhorn to use her charms on a couple of men sitting at a table in the corner.

Colbry was disappointed that the man he was jawing with didn't seem to see his friends in the establishment.

"Where are your two partners anyway?" asked Colbry.

The man shrugged. "I—I ain't got no partners. If you think I done something to you, go tell it to the law."

"That would be a waste of time, wouldn't it. Now I'm going outside. You better come with me. If you do I'll let you go fetch your friends. If you don't, I'll be back in five minutes and I'll kill you where you stand."

Unnerved, the man looked around at the other patrons. "You heard him! He threatened to murder me! Someone fetch the sheriff, pronto!"

The others looked at him and then at Colbry. No one moved toward the door. No one except Colbry, who turned his back on the man and walked outside. He crossed the street and leaned against a post on the boardwalk of the building facing the saloon. When the bushwhacker emerged from the Buckhorn he hovered just outside the door, warily scanning the street. When he spotted Colbry he turned to go back inside the cantina then changed his mind and hurried eastward down the street. Colbry didn't go after him. He pulled a cheroot from his shirt pocket, scraped a strike-anywhere on the post, and lit it up. The sun was much higher in the sky now, and beads of sweat appeared on his brow, but he didn't step back into the shade. He was accustomed to heat thanks to his years fighting the Apaches. He wasn't sure if the bushwhacker and his cohorts would face him. It was possible they would make a run for it. But Colbry wasn't worried about that, either. He didn't doubt that he could track them down.

He was a little surprised when the belligerent Ben Mackey found him not ten minutes later. "What the hell are you doing in town, Colbry?"

"Looking for the men who bushwhacked Laurie Ruston."

Mackey was surprised. "Is she dead?"

Colbry shook his head. "She's on the right side of the grass."

"These men, who are they?"

"Don't know their names. Names don't matter anyway."

"Then how will you know who did it?"

"Because I saw three men watching your office when Laurie and I showed up to bail out Jim Street. Then later that day three men ambushed us. This morning I tracked three horses from the woods where they tried their bushwhacking. They led me here."

The sheriff scowled. "Could've been three other men. You got no proof…"

"Yes I do."

"Then tell me what it is."

Again, Colbry shook his head. "Unless they come at me with guns barking, I'll have them show me their horses. Then I'll know for sure."

"And how is that, pray tell."

"One of them was poorly shod."

"And if they don't you'll just gun 'em down," said Mackey.

"If they don't show me their horses then I reckon so. But it'll be self-defense, won't it?"

"I don't follow."

"Like you, they'll think I spotted their horses at the ambush site. Or one of them anyway."

Mackey glared a moment longer, pushing his lips out and then pulling them in several times, picking his words carefully. "I'll have my eye on you, Colbry. You're trouble. And if you kill a man in cold blood I'll see you hanged."

Colbry's eyes were as cold as blue ice. "When you want to try that, bring help," he suggested, and walked away.

Chapter Eleven

Colbry took the sheriff's threat seriously. Many were the times his life had been in danger, but that had never stopped him from doing what needed to be done. Worrying about what could go wrong was an indulgence that only increased the likelihood that it would go wrong.

He figured the men he was hunting would do one of two things. Come for him or run away, and he didn't have to wait long to find out which. He strolled down to the next building and found another post to lean against, so that the sun was behind him. Ten minutes after Mackey left him, he saw all three of the bushwhackers coming down the boardwalks on the other side of the street, toward the Buckthorn. The one Colbry had confronted earlier waited outside while the other two entered the saloon. It didn't take long for the first man to locate Colbry across the street. He hurried inside to tell his partners and a minute later all three of them were standing on the boardwalk, looking across at him. They conferred briefly, then stepped out into the street. The paunchy man in the middle carried a sawed-off shotgun. He flashed a mirthless grin at Colbry.

"Hear tell you're looking for us, cowboy," he hollered from forty feet away.

That made other people on the street begin to scatter, ducking through doors or into alleys. Colbry pushed off the post and stepped out into the street. A cross-street shooting spree could end up with dead or wounded horses, not to mention bystanders. People began ducking into buildings and alleys as Colbry closed the distance with the trio by about fifteen feet. The hustle and bustle of the thriving town suddenly stopped, replaced by a hushed, palpable tension. His flanking movement turned the trio, making them look eastward. The sun was high in the morning sky, so it was behind Colbry – and in the eyes of the three ambushers.

"That's right," said Colbry. "I want to see your horses."

The three men exchanged puzzled looks. Then the man in the middle brayed a derisive laugh. "What are you, a horse thief?" He laughed at the attempt at humor, while his companions smiled. But their eyes revealed how nervous they were.

"You've got three choices," said Colbry calmly. "Show me your horses, turn tail and run, or die here in the dirt."

"That's pretty bold talk from someone who's outnumbered three to one. I'll give you two choices, mister. You either get on your horse and ride like hell out of Lampasas, or die where you stand."

The bushwhackers on each side of the shotgunner took a step or two away from their leader. Colbry felt a sudden calm overtake him. His heartbeat was slow and steady. He didn't fret over the possibility of dying. He had no emotion at all. He was solely focused on the mechanics of what he was about to do. Keeping an eye on the shotgun, he had a second's forewarning that the fight was on. Before the shotgun boomed he was diving to the left, rolling on his shoulder and fired from the hip the instant he came up on one knee. The bullet struck the shotgunner in the chest and knocked him backward off his feet. The other two men were shooting now and Colbry felt himself struck, which threw his left shoulder back, but he didn't fall; he got to his feet and stepped to his left and, raising his right arm, calmly aimed at one of the pistoleers and put a bullet in his brain. The man remained upright for a second, dying with a surprised expression frozen on his face. As he stumbled backward and then toppled forward onto his face, Colbry fanned the trigger of his .45 Schofield, cutting down the last man, two slugs making him perform a jerky dance before his legs gave out and he sat down hard. His head slumped forward, and death rattled in his throat as life left him.

Colbry holstered his pistol and grabbed his left arm, holding it tight against his side, experiencing the searing heat in his shoulder beginning to spread like wildfire through him. A bit dizzy and unsteady on his feet, he wanted to sit down, but then he saw Mackey appear. The Lampasas lawman gave the three bushwhackers a cursory check, then came closer to Colbry.

"You killed them all," rasped Mackey..

"I know."

"Give me that hogleg of yours."

Colbry looked at the pistol in his hand, but instead of surrendering it to the sheriff he holstered it. "They drew first. I know you want to get paid. So arrest me. But I reckon when you search these men, or their belongings, you'll have a pretty good payday, even after the undertaker gets his cut."

Mackey gave him an ugly look, then glanced around at the gathering of Lampasas citizens. He had to assume that some of them had heard every word Colbry had said.

"Looked like a fair fight to me," said a man in the crowd, and there were heads nodding and murmurs of agreement.

"Yeah and don't forget the horses and tack," said another, sarcastically. "This is a big payday for you, sheriff."

Mackey pursed his lips, glared at Colbry a moment, then growled, "Get out of my town."

"It's our town, too, sheriff," commented the man who had spoken first.

Colbry half turned away, remembered something, and turned back. "Almost forgot. One of their horses had a half-baked shoeing. Might want to fix that before you sell it or folks might get the wrong idea."

Then he turned away, and the crowd parted respectfully as he made his way to the nearby buckskin. But he didn't make it. Blood had drenched his shirt sleeve and was dripping from the numbed fingers of his left arm. Suddenly he felt very light-headed and the world began to spin a little and then tilt. A man saw him stumble and leaped forward to prevent him from falling.

"Someone help me get him to the doc!" he bellowed and two more men came up to assist in helping Colbry off the street.

He was barely aware of going inside the doctor's office, and of being helped into a back room and laid out on a narrow bed. The ceiling was spinning and he heard a man say, "He is losing a lot of blood. Someone cut that sleeve off!" Colbry glimpsed a narrow, sallow face adorned with a trim mustache and goatee and eyes filled with concern. "The bullet missed the bone and went right through, but he's bleeding badly…" Colbry groaned as a tourniquet was pulled agonizingly tight. The ceiling began to spin. He closed his eyes and passed out.

Mary Keyes was in her room at the Palace Hotel in Lampasas when she heard the shooting in the street. She had been laying in the bed, suffering from the heat even with the room's single window open, and when the gunfire erupted she jumped up and went to the window to see what was going on. She saw three men lying motionless in the street, and she knew them by their clothing to be the ones she and her brother had run into up in the Territories. Then she spotted Colbry near his buckskin house, suddenly stumble and fall. He was quickly hidden from view by townspeople who gathered around him.

Her mind racing, her pulse pounding in her veins, she was sitting on the edge of the bed and had just put on her shoes when Luther burst into the room. In her current state she shrieked and then put a hand over her pounding heart. She took one look at her brother's expression and realized he was as scared as she was.

"We have to get out of here," she said.

Luther closed the door, locked it, and strode to the window. "We should've slipped away after we found out that the ambush failed," he muttered. Then he turned to face Mary. "They were talking about coming up here and…" He shook his head. He knew he didn't need to finish the sentence. "I talked them out of it. Told them the Ruston woman would probably come to town to report it to the law, and Colbry might come with her. So they agreed to wait one day." He glanced out the window again. "But now they're dead. Nothing will happen to you now."

Mary was furious. She got to her feet, took two steps to come face to face with her brother and slapped him, hard.

"We should have left last night," she said, her voice shrill. "No. No, we should have gone back east as soon as we were chased out of Ellsworth! But no! You and you're injured pride. We could have been murdered when we met those … those jackals! I could have been raped! I'm glad they're dead!"

She was shouting at the top of her lungs now and Luther grabbed her by the shoulders and gave her a shake. "Keep your voice down and your wits about you!" He pushed her back until she was sitting on the edge of the bed again, then sat beside her and put an arm around her shoulders. Tears were streaming down her cheeks and he fished a handkerchief out of the pocket of his jacket and wiped them away. He sat there a moment, rubbing his chin and collecting his thoughts.

"What are we going to do?" she asked. "Where are we going to go? If Colbry finds us in Lampasas he'll think we had something to do with those bastards. Oh my god, I am glad they are dead but…but what do we do now? Colbry is a stone cold killer!"

"We'll ride to San Antonio," said Luther, having fashioned a spur-of-the-moment plan. "We can catch a stage east from there. I know! We can go to New Orleans. Plenty of gambling joints. We'll have good luck there. I can feel it in my bones. We'll make lots of money. And you can buy the best clothes there. The newest fashions. Drink coffee in the cafes along the river. Then…then, if we want, we can ride steamboats up and down the Mississippi River and make more money still. Colbry will never find us. We'll put him and all the rest of this far behind us. What do you say, sis?"

She used a lace-trimmed handkerchief to dab at her eyes. "You promise? I mean the part about putting Colbry behind us. You can put aside your thirst for vengeance?"

"To hell with him. He was wounded in the shootout. For all I know, he's hurt badly and won't live to see the sun rise tomorrow. I'm done with him and with this country. Let's go back to where people are civilized."

Mary managed a smile and nodded. She had visions of sitting on the deck of a riverboat adorned in the latest fashions and flirting with true gentlemen as she sipped mint julips. "How far way is San Antonio?"

"About three days ride."

Mary fell back on the bed with a sigh of vast relief. "I can't wait," she murmured.

"This is becoming a habit."

Colbry opened his eyes and saw Laurie Ruston's face. She was standing beside the bed, clad in a white shirt tucked into brown riding britches which were, he assumed, tucked into riding boots. He didn't feel like rolling over to the side of the bed and looking down at her feet. She was gazing at him and for an instant he wondered why, then turned his head left and then right and realized he was laying on his back in a narrow bed, covered by a blanket, in a small room separated by an open doorway from what was clearly a doctor's office. There were glass-fronted cabinets along two walls, their upper shelves lined with labeled bottles and can-isters, and a small curtained window in the back wall, above his head. Through the doorway he could see a desk and a few chairs and a couple of bookcases laden with tomes.

An intense and steady, throbbing pain emanated from his left arm and then he remembered why. His shirt was off so he could study the very professional dressing that covered his arm from the elbow up and also his shoulder. His throat was as dry as a desert and he licked his lips. Laurie half turned and poured some water from a pitcher into a glass, put her hand behind his head and lifted it slightly as she put the rim of the glass to his lips. He gulped down every drop.

"Doc Seymour is busy tending to the men you shot down," said Laurie. "He doubles as the coroner in

Lampasas, apparently. We had another coroner when I was just a child, but I think he was shot and killed by a half-breed drunk who had made a name for himself taking the scalps of every man he put down, and who thought, in his inebriated state, that the coroner was taking the scalps he thought were his by right. Anyway, Doc says the bullet grazed an artery, so you bled a lot. The doc says I can take you home tomorrow but the next day would be better, and that you need a week or two of bedrest. I will put you in a room in the big house so that Alonso and I can keep an eye on you."

"Don't need a couple of days," replied Colbry, his voice rough and croaky, and as if to prove his point he tried to get up on his good arm's elbow, then gasped as bolts of red hot pain shot through his shoulder, taking his breath away.

"Men are silly," murmured Laurie. "Would you like some morphine? Doc left a bottle right over there and said I could give you some if you came to. But I don't know why I asked. You're going to say no."

He lay down gingerly and wheezed. "You're right. Some years back I was shot in the leg by an Apache broncho who also killed my horse. I had to walk a couple days back to Fort Union. The only good thing that came of it was my next horse was Boots. Point is, I can handle the pain."

"You are such a hardcase. How does a man become such a tough hombre?"

He studied her face, wondering if she was being sarcastic, but it was clear that she meant it as a genuine compliment. "You'd do the same. We only have one life to live and most folks will do whatever they can to hold onto it." He tried to lighten the mood since she looked so serious. "Anyway, you always wanted me under your roof." She was still pretty when frowning, but prettier when she smiled, and he was trying to make her smile. "I'll pay the sawbones, and the expense of burying those men, too."

"No, you won't. I already took care of all that. You work for me. I will always buy Rocking Chair cowboys out of the hoosegow and pay the sawbones to heal them when they have wounds Alonzo and I can't handle because I need them to do their jobs, not lay about in bed."

"And your excuse for burying those damn ambushers?"

Laurie shrugged. "Just cleaning up the mess one of my hands made. I expect it might not be the last time."

"Take it out of my pay."

"Hush. I will do no such thing."

"What about Mackey? I'm surprised he doesn't want to lock me up, just so you'll pay him to let me out."

Laurie smirked and shook her head. "He isn't going to do anything except let Barrett Faulkner know his hired gun hands are eating dirt."

"You think Faulkner hired those men?"

She settled in a ladderback chair beside the bed, rubbing the back of her neck. Suddenly tired and partly from the worry over Colbry, she rested the back of her head against the top rail of the rocker. "Sure he did. Who else could it be? Faulkner wants the Rocking Chair. And if something happens to me … Well, I am the last Ruston. Hence the ambush."

"Maybe you should get married and have a passel of younguns."

This time she tilted her head a little sideways and smiled wryly at him. "Are you proposing?"

"Uh … well no. I was just saying …"

Laurie laughed softly at his flustered look, and then pouted for effect. "Darn."

Colbry felt his cheeks warm and realized that for perhaps the first time in his adult life he was blushing. He noticed for the first time that the curtains on the small window above his head were moving because the window was open to let some of the heat that accumulated during the long summer day escape and he could tell for the first time that it was night. He touched his face and said, "Was it you who shaved me?"

Laurie nodded. "You looked like a bum and..."

"Don't say it. You don't want your cowhands to look like bums."

She laughed softly, a soft, lilting laugh that was music to his ears. "As for our distinguished local lawman, he should come by and thank you. After all, he has the horses and all the gear those three men owned that he can eventually sell. Notice has to be put in the newspaper but those men aren't from around here so if they have any kin the notice won't be seen by them and their belongings won't be claimed."

"And if there is anything in their belongings that could connect them to Faulkner, the sheriff can make sure it isn't seen by anyone."

"You have a suspicious mind."

"Wouldn't surprise me if Faulkner was behind the disappearance of your father, not the Comanches."

Laurie no longer looked light-hearted. For a moment she was silent, and Colbry feared he had stepped over a line.

"Well," she said, in a subdued voice, "Maybe I should take your advice, then. Find a good man and bear a couple of children." She elevated her chin and looked at him with features as emotionless as that of a cigar store's wooden Indian. "Hurry up and heal. I need you to get back to work."

And with that she walked out of the room, into the physician's office and out into the street.

Two days later, first thing in the morning, Colbry had another visitor: Burr Welken.

"I rode back to the ranch house from the line shack with bad news, and found out you'd been wounded in a gunfight in that street out yonder," said Burr.

Colbry said it was so and, while tersely recounting the event, suggested that the three men he had gunned down most likely worked for Faulkner.

"Wouldn't surprise me," said Burr. "Three men, you say. If you keep that up, Cordell, you're going to be the subject of your own dime novel. You happen to know where I might find the boss lady?"

"She's at the hotel, as far as I know. Did something happen? Why are you looking for her?"

"Well, as you know, it'll be time before too much longer to go out and start branding cattle for the drive next spring. So I was roaming the brasada trying to find out where they've been grazing when I saw some sign that made me think a bunch of them had fallen into the hands of rustlers. Eighty, maybe a hundred head, pushed south by west. I followed the trail and sure 'nuff they were herded off of Rocking Chair land."

Colbry fumed. He managed to sit up and then swung his legs off one side and, looking around at Burr, grumbled, "Sounds like Tom Selman and his bunch are at it again. I should have shot them down when I had the chance. Where are my damn boots?"

"Whoa, pardner. Too soon for you to go galloping across the plains. You might start bleeding again, and then it'll be hell to pay. Miss Ruston would lay into me with a vengeance if I let you do that in your condition. I'm gonna go find her and give her the news. Maybe I'll stop by the Buckhorn and have a quick drink of whiskey first. Or two." A broad grin furrowed his sun-dark cheeks and he put a hand on Colbry's good shoulder. "You just settle down. The more rest you get, the sooner you can start looking to get shot up again."

Not long after, Burr returned, and this time he was accompanied by Laurie. The doctor had just arrived to check on Colbry, and was changing the dressing on his arm. When asked for his assessment of Colbry's condition and when he could be taken back to the Rocking Chair, the doctor pondered a moment, lips pursed, then answered.

"Well, based just on the scars I can see on his upper torso, this fellow has been shot and knifed more often than most men his age, so I suppose he can handle the discomfort. Come get him tomorrow, Miss Ruston, and take him home. I'll give you what you need to change the dressing every day or two, and a sling, as well. He shouldn't use that arm for a while. If he starts bleeding again it will be arterially, and he could die." His bushy brows furrowed as he looked at his patient. "As for you, sir, rest that arm for a couple of weeks." Reading Colbry's expression, he added, "Or a week at least. Give yourself to help up."

"Not to worry, doc," said Laurie. "We've got a rocking chair in deep shade back at the ranch, and he can spend his days there." She turned to Welken. "Burr, you can go back to the ranch and take care of things. I'll stay here tonight and rent a buckboard from the livery and bring Cordell home tomorrow."

Burr frowned. "You sure you don't want an escort? I mean, after all, it wasn't too long ago you got bushwhacked."

"I'm handy enough with a rifle," said Laurie, then pointed at Colbry. "And there's nothing wrong with his gun arm. We'll be okay."

"Yes, ma'am." He touched the brim of his hat, then gave Colbry a nod before walking out onto the street.

Laurie settled in a chair near the window, watching the back and forth flow of people on the street and the boardwalks. She didn't speak while the doc tended to a man who walked in with a cough and raw throat, and after the sawbones had made up a tonic for his new patient, he took off his white tunic and showed up in the doorway between the two halves of his office.

"Zeke Randall's wife is getting close to birthing her fourth child, and I need to go out and check on her," he told Laurie. "Make sure your cowboy stays off his feet, if you would, Miss Ruston. If he moves too much he'll open up that wound and start bleeding again. I would suggest he stays out of the saddle for at least a week." His expression made it manifestly apparent that he expected his advice to be ignored.

Laurie promised she would make sure of it, and the doctor left. Colbry grimaced. Laying around like an invalid for even a few hours, much less a day or two, rubbed him the wrong way, but he didn't say anything since he was past ready to get out of the doctor's office and back on his feet.

"I've been in worse shape," he groused.

"I'm sure. But I need you in good health and back in the saddle as soon as possible." She looked out the window again, her chin resting on her cupped hand, a thoughtful expression on her face. A moment later she stood up and said, "I'm going to go make sure there will be a buckboard available to us in the morning. You stay put. If you get up and open that wound I'm going to start docking your pay."

"Yes, ma'am," said Colbry, amused in spite of his situation. Then he wondered if she would actually carry out the threat.

As usual, Colbry awoke before sunrise, and found himself alone in the back room of the doctor's office. He had gone to sleep with Laurie seated in a chair, reading from a small book of poetry which she had fished out of her saddlebags. But she was gone now, and then he remembered why. The physician was in the other room, sitting at his desk, asleep. He could smell coffee and saw a pot steaming on top of an old cast-iron stove behind the desk. Colbry was successful in getting out of bed and standing up, though the pain was still intense and he was light-headed for a moment. His clothes were on a chair in the corner, neatly folded, and he had managed to get his canvas pants on when he heard the buckboard out in the street and then Laurie exhorting the pair of mules in the traces to come to a stop. Colbry had managed to sit up by the time she came inside. Her entrance woke the doctor and he offered her some coffee but she declined, then asked after his patient. By that time the sawbones had glimpsed Colbry in the other room gingerly putting on his shirt.

"Well I guess you might as well take him, Miss Ruston. He isn't going to stay in bed and heal up, apparently. I expected that to be the case, so I made a basket of dressings and a vial of carbolic acid for you to take with you. It's over there on my desk. That carbolic acid works as an antiseptic, and I advise you to clean the wound and redress it twice a day. You have no idea how significantly that British doctor, Lister, changed medicine with his discovery of the benefits of carbolic acid. There is some opium powder in there, too, if the pain becomes too severe. Just use it sparingly, as the addiction will ruin any man."

Laurie promised to rely sparingly on the powder, and said that she had some idea about carbolic acid, since she had used it now and again on injured horses, Then she went into the backroom and helped Colbry finish buttoning his shirt. The doctor helped him get his boots on. Colbry hated being so incapacitated that he couldn't even get dressed on his own. Laurie and the doctor steadied him as he walked through the office and out into the golden morning sunlight casting long blue shadows along the street. Laurie had bought some saddle blankets and laid them out in the back of the buckboard but Colbry adamantly shook his head.

"I am done being on my back," he groused.

The physician frowned and shook his head, but Laurie smiled warmly.

"Then travel beside me," she said, and climbed onto the bench and gathered up the team's rein leather, waiting until Colbry, one-handed, managed to climb up beside her. The sawbones didn't help him what that, and Colbry assumed the man was drawing the line when it came to assisting suicide. Laurie slapped the reins against the backsides of the mules and they were off, the slowly rising sun warm on their backs.

Chapter Twelve

That night Colbry slept in one of the guest rooms in the big house. Though he assured Laurie that his bed in the bunkhouse was just fine she would have none of it, and he had to admit that the bed he ended up in was the most comfortable that he could remember having ever experienced in his life. Which, considering his service in the war between the states, followed by his years of work as an army scout, during which he slept on a blanket spread out on the ground for weeks if not months at a time, would not have surprised anyone.

The next day Laurie assigned Colbry to a rocking chair in the shade of the ranch house courtyard and he didn't like that at all because cowboys would come and go pretty regularly on business. Most would tell him how glad they were that he was back. But he felt like he was on display and it made him uncomfortable, especially since he was sitting in deep shade sipping water while all the Rocking Chair cowboys who came to see him would end up hot, tired and dirty after a long summer day's labor.

His first morning back on the ranch, Laurie woke him with a breakfast of ham and eggs and fresh coffee and he was rather ashamed being served breakfast in bed but he had to admit that it was much tastier than the bean soup he had been given while laid up, wounded, in a bed at Fort

Bowie following an Apache ambush. He made the mistake of telling Laurie this, and then had to tell the whole story.

"It was near Apache Pass, and one of the few forts that at that time had stone walls. It was a Butterfield stage station at first. Even had gunports in the mule corral. The stage company used mules; you pretty much had to, out there in that country. But the Butterfield Stage Company didn't last long. I was a private in a detachment commanded by a Lieutenant Bascom, who was ordered to find and recover a young white boy stolen by Cochise's Apaches. It was 1861. At the time there was an uneasy peace with the Apaches, but Bascom ruined that.

"He arranged a meeting with Cochise, the chief of the Chiricahua Apache to negotiate for the release of the boy. But then he got it in his head to hold Cochise hostage. And while Bascom did get his hands on a couple of Apaches, Cochise escaped. You see, as it turned out, Cochise didn't have the boy, and he had told Bascom as much, but the lieutenant didn't believe him. So Cochise and his warriors surrounded the station and started firing on us from the hills and ravines. It was impossible to tell how many. Somehow we managed to hold out. I was shot in the thigh on the last day of the siege."

Laurie asked him how long the siege had lasted.

"Sixteen days. Longest sixteen days of my life. I'm surprised we held out. Only forty men in the detachment when the shooting started." Colbry's features were bleak as he remembered. "It was bad. Some of the soldiers were captured and tortured. I can still hear their screams. But then some Apaches tried to get too close and they were captured, too. Those warriors were executed on the spot." He shook his head, then pulled himself out of the past and looked at her. "That was a big mistake. I told Bascom that, but he wouldn't listen. People say that's what started the Apache Wars. It also put an end to the Butterfield Stage Company, since after that it was open season on those stagecoaches for the Apaches."

"So did you ever think about staying in the Army?"

"Not a chance. I scouted for them for a few years, then I went north into the mountains, where they were finding gold. But I didn't find much. I wandered down to the border and worked on a ranchero run by Don Pablo Reynosa. Then I left that job too."

"Why?"

"I made a mistake," said Colbry, cursing himself for even bringing it up. He'd had sense enough not to while traveling with Laurie all the way down to Texas from Ellsworth.

Laurie studied his face for a moment, a faint smile on her lips, head slightly tilted to one side. "You don't have to tell me if you don't want to. But I don't think you would commit murder, or engage in rustling. Or am I reading you wrong?"

He shook his head. "No, nothing like that. Worse."

Laurie's eyes widened and she sat forward in the chair she had placed beside the bed, elbows on knees, hands clasped. "Let me guess. You bedded your employer's daughter? Or his wife"

"Daughter."

"What was her name?"

Colbry was surprised by the question, and wondered why Laurie wanted to know. He had to put it down to one of the many mysteries that the female of the species held for him. They could keep secrets from you and wax indignant if pressed, but God help you if you didn't provide all the facts about your own transgressions. "Sombra was her name."

"Did you ... make her with child?"

"Nope. But she was a rebel. Didn't like the way her father protected her. She had a hot temper, and she and her father would often get into arguments, sometimes about his plans for her. You see, down there, sometimes fathers marry off their daughters for advantage. Could be political, or about business. And virginity was a big selling point."

"That's not much different from the way some fathers back East conduct their family affairs, mused Laurie."

"Anyway, at one point she told him what had happened, just to hurt him, I suppose."

Laurie's eyes narrowed suspiciously. "Didn't you know about those traditions? Or did you just not care about them? Maybe she was in love with you. Did you love her?"

Colbry shrugged, then winced as the ill-advised movement tweaked his wound. "I don't know." He glanced at her, embarrassed. And, since he couldn't remember ever experiencing embarrassment, he tried to make a joke, which turned out to be a lame one. "Honestly, I'm not even sure if I would know love if it hit me in the face with a skillet."

She looked at him in a way that made him a little uncomfortable. It was as though she could see right down into his soul. "From what you've told me, I would say you've had a pretty lonesome life. You need a place you can call home. I'm glad my father was smart enough to hire you on. I'm glad you're here. I would like it very much if someday you would consider the Rocking Chair your home. It's time you had one. It's time you had people around you that cared about your well-being."

He didn't know how to respond to that, so all he did was nod. But Laurie wasn't done. She stood there in front of him, hands on hips, her gaze steady and piercing.

"You know, life is full of promise and disappointment. I think there isn't much a person can do about the latter. The promise you have to seize before it passes you by. But you can't or won't if you don't think you're worthy of the good things in life."

There came the sudden clamor of the dinner triangle from the direction of the kitchen. Laurie smiled.

"Alonzo does love ringing that bell," she commented, amused. "I'll bring you a plate if you like."

"No, I'll go to the table, but thanks." Colbry eased himself out of the rocking chair, felt an intense twinge in his left arm but stood up anyway and walked with Laurie across the shade-speckled courtyard.

Meals were taken at a very long table in the very long dining room connected by a door to Alonso's domain, the kitchen. Sixteen people could sit at the table and fourteen did that day: Laurie and Colbry and twelve other cowboys. The conversation started off with Colbry being the topic, and several cowboys took good-natured jabs at him. "What do you know, Cordell got himself shot just in time, now that we're sweating up a storm gathering up the unbranded cows!" And another chimed in with "I hear tell he walked into the bullet on purpose, being the tough hombre that he is, just so's he could live in the big house a while."

Colbry laughed at the ribbing and then engaged in ranch talk with the cowboys for the rest of the dinner, since they had been riding the range while he had been riding a bed and the rocking chair that Laurie soon suggested that he occupy again. He spent some of the long afternoon sitting in that chair thinking about what she had said. The promise you have to seize before it passes you by. But you can't or won't if you don't think you're worthy of the good things in life. He wondered if Laurie was right. Had he wandered all his adult life because he didn't think he deserved any better?

After another interminable afternoon of sitting in a rocking chair, Laurie showed up to inform him that she had cooked supper for them both. This revelation just enhanced a nagging worry that some of the other ranch hands might start to resent him for being on the receiving end of special treatment. Laurie could sense his reservations and told him to consider it a working supper, and they spent an hour discussing what it would take to transform the mustangs they had gathered into good working horses. She then asked him to take charge of that job.

"I'll send someone out to the western line shack and bring Burr in to take charge of the branding," she said. "Beholden will produce a special breed of horse, Cord. In a few years I would like it widely known that the Rocking Chair has the best horses in Texas. Eventually we'll buy or build an office and stable in San Antonio devoted entirely to that enterprise. What do you think?"

Colbry thought it over and chose his words carefully. "I think it's what you've dreamed of doing and so if you don't do it you'll be wondering if you should have until the day you die."

Laurie smiled pensively. "But you don't think it's a good idea, do you? Or at least you think it's risky."

Colbry put his knife and fork down and settled back in the high-backed chair, his steak and potato half-eaten. A full minute passed while he mulled it over, then shook his head. "There's always a risk. But Texas is growing, and growing fast. More and more people will be pushing west, into Comancheria, and they will need good horseflesh. A lot of the will pass through San Antonio on the way. Most of them will be wanting to raise cattle and they will need a lot of good horses to help them do that job. You're looking ahead and your vision is keen."

She looked very pleased. A few minutes later, when they were done with the main meal, she carried the plates away and returned with an apple pie which she announced she had made that day. It wasn't long out of the oven. After consuming his slice of pie, Colbry wasn't lying when he proclaimed it the best pie he had ever tasted.

To top off the feast, Laurie produced a bottle of French cognac. "I think my mother was responsible for the very cosmopolitan liquor cabinet I discovered when I got home."

The cognac was an explosion of warm nectar with a cherry aftertaste on Colbry's uncultured palate, and by the time he had finished his glass he was feeling very relaxed and drowsy. He thanked her for the meal – the best meal he had ever had, he declared – and offered to help clear the table, but Laurie would hear none of it and sent him to bed.

After a day of lounging in the shade and a big supper topped off with cognac, Colbry sighed with contentment when he stretched out on his bed. He was asleep in no time. But as usual he was a light sleeper, and the creak of a loose floorboard brought him fully awake, his eyes flashing open as he reached for the Schofield pistol in the gun belt dangling from the left-side bed post. The room was dark, but not entirely; moonlight was slipping through the curtains half-closed over the window. Going for the pistol produced a sharp stab of pain in his shoulder, enough to make him gasp. Then Laurie stepped into the dim moonlight filtering through the window curtains.

"Don't shoot," she said calmly. "If you kill me, you're out of a job."

Colbry put both shoulders back on the mattress with an audible sigh of relief. "Might want to knock on the door next time."

"I just wanted to check on you." Laurie settled on the edge of the bed and Colbry took notice that she wore a light pink robe with embroidered shoulders over her night clothes. "I'm sorry if I hurt you."

"It's nothing."

"I expect there is a key to the door…somewhere. I'll look for it."

"Don't bother. It's your home. I'm just visiting. I'll be back in the bunkhouse before you know it."

Laurie braced herself by reaching across to put her hand on the other side of him and leaned forward. "Maybe," she murmured. "But I wouldn't count on it." And then she kissed him on the lips, a short, soft, but passionate kiss that took his breath away. Then she slipped off the bed. "Now go back to sleep."

Colbry gazed at her, intoxicated by her scent, his lips still tingling from her kiss, and doubted he would sleep much now, thanks to her. She paused at the door to look back at him, a vision of softly smiling loveliness and long- ing – a vision he knew he would keep for the rest of his days.

He lay awake most of the night, mulling over what had just happened, and harkened back to the time when Laurie had asked him about his sojourn with Sombra, the daughter of Don Pablo Reynosa, and whether he made her with child. Odds were that had he done so he would have been killed and the baby given to some peasant family. It occurred to him that while she hadn't said it straight out, Laurie was thinking about having an heir, so that the Rocking Chair Ranch would remain in Ruston hands when she had passed on. And either he was flattering himself or it was pretty clear that she was considering his worthiness to be the sire.

It was exactly the kind of situation he had run away from more than once in his travels. He had never considered himself good material for settling down and raising a family, and always told himself he was doing a favor to the handful of women he had come to know by just riding away when the time seemed right. But he knew down deep that wasn't the reason. His father's death by a Mexican firing squad and his mother struck down by pneumonia had broken his heart, and he had never wanted to take a chance of hurting like that again by committing himself to a relationship. It was a pain deeper and more profound than any broken bone or bullet wound.

But he couldn't get past the vivid memory of how Laurie Ruston had looked a few moments ago. Her intoxicating scent still inhabited his nostrils. His lips still seemed to tingle from her kiss. He vividly remembered how he felt the first time he had laid eyes on her, when she was coming down the long staircase at the Drovers Cottage hotel in Ellsworth. She wasn't the most beautiful woman he had ever seen but there was something about her that many other women he knew lacked, a combination of self-confidence and determination mingled with a natural grace and beauty. This made Laurie irresistible.

And so he wondered. Wondered if the reason he had never put down roots was because he hadn't met her yet.

The next evening after supper, when she came to his room again, dressed as before, in that soft robe over her night clothes, he seized her arm with his right hand and pulled her down on top of him and kissed her, a kiss to which she responded with fervor and a quiet little moan of desire, her lithe body moving needily on top of his. They broke the kiss for breath and she smiled a smile that was both sweet and salacious.

"Am I to take it you aren't leaving?"

"No, ma'am. I'm thinking I'm staying here, if it's okay with you."

Laurie smiled the biggest, brightest smile he had ever seen.

"You have no idea how 'okay' it is."

And that was all the talking they did for hours.

The next morning, as the dawn light was creeping through the window curtains, Colbry woke and, still groggy from a deep sleep, groped across the bed for Laurie. Failing to find her, he pried his eyes open, raised his head, and was relieved and happy to see her across the way, sitting in the room's only chair. But his happiness waned when he registered her expression. She had been staring at the ceiling, her head resting on the back of the chair, a solemn expression on her face. When he stirred she lifted her head and brushed her long, tousled brown hair away from her face and smiled warmly, then rose and crossed the room. The robe hung open and he saw that she was naked underneath. She sat on the edge of the bed, and laid a hand light as a feather on his chest.

"You slept well," she murmured.

"Well, as they say, I was rode hard and put up wet," he said, expecting the risqué reply to elicit a laugh. But Laurie's smile was pensive. Colbry stopped smiling. "What's the matter? Regrets?"

She shook her head and brushed wayward strands of hair away from her face. "I was just thinking about something."

"About what?"

"Those three men you killed. The ones that bushwhacked us. We both know Barrett Faulkner put them up to it. He has the most to gain if I end up dead. Question is, what do we do about it?"

Colbry sighed. His morning-after contentment was gone. "I reckon I need to kill him first."

"That could start a bloody range war. He has a son."

"Sometimes it doesn't matter how big the fight is," said Colbry. "You have to take it on."

When they reached the town of Austin, which more or less marked the halfway point between Lampasas and the city of San Antonio, Luther Keyes was relieved. He and Mary had come across a peddler in a mule-drawn wagon which was filled with all manner of items that the man tried to sell to folks living out in the country, ranging from pots and pans to tonics and clothing and even musical instruments like fiddles and mouth organs. The peddler remarked that he was happy for the company, especially since he had heard tell of a band of Indians that had been seen roaming the area, though as far as he knew no homestead or traveler had been accosted. The peddler was a fount of information regarding the area, as he had been plying his trade for nigh on twenty years.

Austin, he said, had started out as a small community on the banks of the Colorado River known as Waterloo some forty years ago. That name amused him, and was why he always liked to give folks he met a little history lesson. But soon Waterloo was renamed Austin in honor of Stephen F. Austin, the Virginia-born visionary who had served as a legislator, a bank director, a newspaper editor, and a circuit court judge. His father, Moses Austin had won an empresarial grant from Spain, which ruled over Mexico. Moses had dreams of leading folks into the promised land like his namesake had, but died before he could realize his dream.. Moses Austin's son was reluctant to become involved with Texas but was persuaded by his mother to finish what his father had started. So Stephen Austin dutifully traveled south to carry out her wishes.

In Louisiana, Austin had the great good fortune of meeting Jose Navarro, an ambitious empresario who was of great help when it came to obtaining empresario contracts. The Spanish governor of Texas allowed Austin to lay claim to land between the Brazos and Colorado rivers, a claim large enough to provide every farming family with one hundred and seventy-seven acres of land and every rancher with over four thousand acres. The Spanish government was hopeful that the settlers, who were required to pledge fealty to the new government, would be of great assistance in battling hostile Indians.

But before Austin could recruit settlers and claim the land, Moses the peddler told the Keyes, he learned that Mexico had gained its independence from Spain and that it's presidente, Agustin de Iturbide, refused to recognize the old land grant, forcing Austin to travel to Mexico City, where he convinced the new government to approve the land grant. Austin went back to Texas but then Iturbide abdicated and the empresarial contract was again rendered null and void. In 1825, the Mexican state of Coahuila y Tejas passed a law that reauthorized the grant for three hundred families, which came to be known as the Old Three Hundred. In the next few years Austin was finally able to bring settlers to the new promised land.

But ten years later Texans had revolted against the rule of Antonio Lopez de Santa Anna and ,who undertook another journey to Mexico to negotiate a peace, was arrested and imprisoned for a year and a half. Once freed, he returned to Texas and was involved in the revolution against the dictator Santa Anna's defeat at San Jacinto and the creation of the Republic of Texas. Austin went to New Orleans to urge the United States to support the Texas cause. After Santa's Anna defeat at San Jacinto, Austin was persuaded to run for President of the new Republic but was defeated by Sam Houston. He accepted the post of Secretary of State but, following a brief illness, died on December 16, 1836, at the age of forty-three.

When the peddler asked Luther Keyes what he did for a living, Keyes told him he was a gambler by trade, and the other man issued a somber warning.

"I ain't got nothing against gamblers, mind you. But mark my words. You'd better not get into any trouble at all in Austin, or take money from the wrong man, 'cause if you do you'll end up on the wrong side of the law and spend a good bit of time on the wrong side of iron bars, too."

Keyes grimaced. "Well, lately Lady Luck has turned her back on me, so I am not surprised."

"On the other hand," said the peddler, "You could head on south to San Antonio. That town is wild and wide open. I expect you would prosper there, and short of shooting someone you ought not to draw the attention of the law."

Keyes nodded and fell silent, deep in thought, grim and brooding. The peddler, who was a skilled reader of people, left him alone with his thoughts. So did Mary. It wasn't until they reached Austin and had parted company with the peddler that she spoke.

"Are we going to San Antonio?" she asked.

"I suppose."

"That's a long way from Lampasas. What about Clay Colbry?"

Keyes shrugged. "Sometimes you just have to fold and walk away from the table."

Mary was pleasantly surprised, and hugged her brother. "Good!" she exclaimed. "Let's get on with our lives. I have a feeling we will fit in nicely down in San Antonio. As for Colbry, he'll get his comeuppance someday."

That night – the first time in Mary's memory that her brother hadn't taken a place at a poker table – they rested up in a hotel room and left Austin at the crack of dawn. At midday they saw smoke rising above the trees. A mile further on they found the source. It was a small cabin with a barn and corrals. The corrals were empty, the gates left open. The barn was burnt rubble, still smoking. The cabin itself had been made of adobe, but the roof, door and window shutters had burned away. A man's body lay in the open doorway, his bare, bloodied legs sticking out over the threshold. Keyes slowed his horse just long enough to look through the open doorway and into the interior shadows of the structure. He saw four arrows embedded in the dead man's chest and his nape hairs crawled. Then Mary, who had ridden past him, shrieked, a hoarse, hollow scream of horror, and Keyes turned to look at her...and then past her at the dead bodies in the deep shade of a big oak tree. The bodies had been stripped naked and mutilated but he thought they had both been women. Or rather one had been a woman and the other a girl. By the size of the latter corpse he guessed the girl had been maybe ten years old. He heard Mary vomiting. Keyes didn't give a thought to giving the dead a decent burial. He grabbed the reins out of his sister's hand and kicked his horse into a canter, leading Mary's mount and putting the cabin and its dead behind.

He calculated that it would take a half day to get back to Austin, but he continued on the way to San Antonio. By nightfall they had reached a creek and made a cold camp there, deciding not to build a fire that might draw unwanted attention. Neither of them slept much, and were in the saddle again before the sun had climbed above the horizon. The country they crossed was mostly rolling prairie with rocky ravines, some of them with water. They steered clear of the small thickets of brush and trees. Luther was becoming more confident about making the journey safely when the band of Comanches suddenly emerged from a ravine not a hundred yards away.

Mary saw them too and screamed a shrill warning and Luther was about to shout at her to ride like hell when he was knocked out of his saddle and found himself lying flat on his back staring up at the blue morning sky, the wind knocked out of him. But it wasn't because of the fall. He stared at the feathered shaft of the arrow protruding from his chest. He couldn't catch his breath and could barely lift his head, but he did so, enough to watch in horror as a Comanche warrior swept Martha out of her saddle. Two of the other braves caught up her horse and Luther's.

With his sister flailing helplessly in the grip of the warrior and screaming hysterically for help as she was carried off into the bushes, Luther managed to get a grip on his pistol and for a split second thought to shoot his own sister, horrified by what he imagined would be done to her. But then a Comanche loomed over him, grinning down at him with eyes that gleamed with savage elation. He grabbed Luther's hair and leaned over, knife in hand. Luther felt the intense pain of the warrior's blade at his hairline as the brave began to take his scalp and, with tears streaming down his cheeks, put the barrel of the pistol to his temple and pulled the trigger.

Chapter Thirteen

Two days later Clay Colbry was standing with Laurie beside him, her arm curled under his, and he was holding her hand, while listening to her recite her marriage vows while gazing up at him.

"I, Laurie Ann Ruston, take thee, Cordell Colbry, to be my husband, to have and to hold from this day forward, for better or for worse, for richer, for poorer, in sickness and in health, to love and to cherish, and I promise to be faithful to you until death parts us."

He was wearing a new shirt, one that Laurie had bought for him in Lampasas the day before, when she had gone into town to talk to the minister. She had bought a new dress, a white one modestly adorned with ribbons and lace. She was radiant with happiness. Colbry gazed into her eyes, the words that passed her lips making him wonder if he was dreaming. That his years of lonely, homeless wandering were a thing of the past was not an easy truth to accept.

The minister, who had been fetched from Lampasas that morning, smiled and nodded at Colbry, who recited the vows. Then the minister solemnly pronounced them man and wife.

More half of the Rocking Chair hands were present, and they cheered and some of them shook Colbry's hands and congratulate Laurie, a few making good-natured jokes as cowboys were wont to do when things got too serious, some of them at the groom's expense, usually focused on his age. but Colbry didn't see even a glimmer of resentment among them, which surprised him, since he was fairly sure that at least a some if not most of the hands were smitten with their boss lady. But then most cowboys just shrugged off disappointment and moved on, because life on the plains was short and not to be wasted moping about what-ifs.

The rest of the hands were out with Burr Welken, whom Laurie had yet to send back to the line rider cabin on the western boundary of the ranch after calling on him to handle the ranch crew during Colbry's recuperation. Burr had been placed in command of a half dozen other cowboys, including Emil Caulfield, who were charged with the task of rousting cattle out of the brasada and then branding them, in preparation for the spring drive. It was Laurie's intention to push at least seven hundred head north to market every spring, steadily diminishing the total number of Rocking Chair cattle.

Meanwhile, the breeding of mares would be the new focus. Beholden was now five years old and was in his prime and could cover up to ten mares in heat every day. Mares could take up to a year to drop a foal and they needed to be at least three or four years old to increase the odds of them safely producing a healthy one. About a dozen of the mustangs that Colbry and the crew had rounded up were male, and half of them were too young to let them breed right away, but there were plenty of mares. All things considered, it was clear that it could take a few years before the horse breeding was going producing at a rate that would satisfy Laurie.

All of this was explained to the ranch hands. Laurie assured them that none would be let go just because there might be, at best, a few hundred cattle grazing Rocking Chair grass in four or five years. Horses would require as much if not more work, and most of the cowboys preferred working with horses anyway. Bronc-busting was more perilous than cow-herding but that fact was appealing to young westerners who were out to prove they had true grit. Some of them, Colbry included, understood the economics of the plan, too. In the long run, the change would improve the odds that the ranch would prosper for decades to come. Once the Comanches were subdued, a big crop of new ranches would hasten the day when the era of the great cattle kings…or queens…came to an end. Until then there would be more cattle ranches in need of good cow ponies.

But first there was the matter of the cattle rustling that Burr Welken had discovered a week ago. The sign that the rustled cattle left behind had led a Rocking Chair scout west and then south, onto Faulkner land. Combined with the rustled cattle Colbry had seen weeks ago while riding the line, that meant almost a couple of hundred cattle had been stolen, and that number was probably higher, maybe quite a bit higher.

The day after the wedding, Colbry awoke to find himself alone in bed. Laurie was standing by the window, watching the morning sky brighten. He rose and walked up behind her, wrapping his arms around her waist and pulling her back into him. She turned her head and he kissed her, a long and passionate kiss that left her breathlessly laughing softly.

"Come back to bed," he said.

She laughed softly, turned around in the circle of his arms, her fingertips playing in his curly chest hair. "We can't stay in bed, cowboy. We have work to do."

It was a gentle chastisement so he persisted, but she slipped out of his embrace. "You're insatiable!" she gasped.

"You're irresistible."

"I'm going to pay Barrett Faulkner a visit."

That dampened his arousal. "Why? What good will that do?" Then he realized it was probably pointless to try to talk her out of it, so he added, "You're not going on your own. I'm going with you." He moved to a chair near the bed, where his clothes were strewn, put on his canvas trousers, then strapped on his gun rig.

"I was going to ask if you didn't volunteer," she replied, smiling. "I'll tell Alonzo what we're doing. If we're not back by tomorrow, he'll know what to do. I mean, if I am to die, I want to die with you. Isn't that romantic? I blame Charlotte Bronte and Jane Austen."

"Who are they?" he asked.

Laurie chuckled. "Authors. You never heard of Pride and Prejudice or Jane Eyre?"

He shook his head. "You're not going to die. Faulker isn't stupid enough to let that happen. He just wants you to give up on the Rocking Chair and go back east."

She nodded, and her expression was evidence that her light-hearted banter was over. "And I want him to know that is never, ever going to happen. If I have to hire fifty more men, the theft of my cattle is going to stop."

Sitting on the chair now, pulling on his socks and stovepipe boots, Colbry gazed at her with wonder. "You're a remarkable woman, Laurie Ruston."

"I'll go get dressed and we'll have breakfast, then ride." She headed for the door and opened it, then turned back before leaving his room. "And my name is Laurie Colbry, by the way." She laughed softly at the sheepish expression on his face and left the room.

The next day they were riding down the road between the big oak trees toward the plantation-style ranch house of Elmwood when a bearded, big-boned man came galloping toward them. Laurie checked her stallion and Colbry turned Boots across her path, putting himself between his wife and the rider. The bearded man checked his horse when he was within speaking distance and touched the brim of his hat, his admiring gaze fastened on Laurie.

"Howdy folks," he drawled. "Name's Merle."

He said no more, clearly expecting them to identify themselves.

"I'm Laurie Colbry. I'm your neighbor. I own the Rocking Chair ranch."

"I thought the Ruston family owned the Rocking Chair."

"I'm the daughter of John Ruston. This is my husband, Cord Colbry."

Merle knew that name, and his bushy brows knit when he fastened a hard gaze on Colbry. He gave a curt nod. "I've heard tell of you. So what brings you here, Mrs. Colbry?"

"I was of a mind to meet my neighbor. Is Mr. Faulkner available?"

Merle tilted his head in the direction of the stately manor further down the road behind him. "He's home." He turned his horse and added, "Come along then."

They rode down the lane and, when they reached the house, dismounted and wrapped their reins around a long hitching pole. A young Mexican woman was emerging from the front door with a basket under her arm, but when she saw them she turned right around and hurried back inside. A moment later Barrett Faulkner emerged on the porch, a smoldering stogie between his fingers producing a wisp of smoke that rose in lazy curlicues on a light summer breeze. His sardonic smile didn't reach his dark eyes when Merle mounted the porch and stepped closer before identifying the two riders he had intercepted.

"John Ruston's daughter is always welcome here," said Faulkner. His gaze shifted to the tall black stallion Laurie had been riding. "A handsome animal you have between your legs, young lady. Please, you are welcome in my house. It's not quite so hot inside."

"I assume my husband is invited, too," said Laurie, with a little gesture at Colbry.

Faulkner was surprised and showed it. "But of course." His gaze swept Colbry from head to toe, a keen appraisal. "I don't believe we've met."

"Name's Colbry."

"I've heard of you, Mr. Colbry. You're the one who had that shootout in the streets of Lampasas. Curled the toes of three men, I hear. Impressive." He turned his attention back to Laurie, looking her over from head to toe as she stepped up onto the porch. "I regret that I missed the wedding, but then I didn't receive an invitation. Please, come inside, both of you. You as well, Merle."

He led the way into the hall and then into the library on the left, and Laurie complimented him on his home. "Reminds me of some of the homes I saw back East."

Faulkner thanked her and entreated them to sit. Laurie settled into a well-cushioned chair, but Colbry remained standing, taking a position behind and little to one side of her, his left hand on the back of the chair, the fingertips of his right hand brushing the hardened leather of his belt holster. He turned a little to his right so that he could better keep an eye on Merle, who remained standing, too, leaning against the side of a bookcase just inside the doorway from the hall. Faulkner offered them a drink but Laurie declined and Colbry didn't say a word. Their host poured himself a glass of brandy and sat in his favorite chair facing them.

"The truth is, Miss Ruston...I mean Mrs. Colbry...I was born poor. My family were Mississippi dirt farmers who never amounted to much. I was determined not to suffer the same fate. So, before the war I came west, staked claim to this land, and ten years later had saved enough money to build this house. Never could have done that in Mississippi, not during Reconstruction, when southerners were punished for wanting to live differently than Yankee merchants."

Laurie scanned the book-laden shelves of the cabinets that lined two walls of the room and said, "You are well-read."

"I had to educate myself."

"Texas has been a new beginning for a lot of people," she said. "A place where they could their dreams. But, of course, that's not what I came to talk to you about."

Faulkner sipped his brandy, peering at her over the rim of the glass with the intensity of a hawk, then chuckled and said, "No, of course not. I didn't think this was a social call."

Laurie was smiling, but there was no warmth in the smile. "A week or so ago one of my men followed the sign of more than a hundred head of Rocking Chair cattle south across Rattlesnake Flats onto your land. There were four or five riders with them. They weren't my riders."

Faulkner friendly smile withered. He took a sip of his brandy, then pursed his lips and fastened a withering gaze on Laurie, the amiable pretense abandoned. "I hope you are not suggesting that I am stealing your cattle. I am sure some of my unbranded cattle wander onto your land. Some of yours wander onto mine. Your father and I had a gentleman's agreement that was based on the logic that it all evened out in the end."

Laurie didn't wither. "Unbranded cattle don't need four or five riders to help them wander across the flats onto your range." She stood up.

"I think I will track those rustlers down," commented Colbry. "I'll find them. You can count on it."

Faulkner scowled and opened his mouth to say something, then changed his mind.

"I won't take up any more of your time, Mr. Faulkner," said Laurie, and stood. "Thank you for your hospitality."

Faulkner put his nearly empty glass of brandy down on the table by his chair and also rose. "I am not a cattle thief," he told her as he managed to put a frosty smile back on his face. "Good day to you both."

Merle showed Laurie and Colbry out. When he returned to the library, Faulkner was pouring himself another brandy.

"I want you to round up all the Rocking Chair cattle we've taken, get fifteen good men, and drive these cows southwest to the Comancheros pronto."

"That could be two hundred head."

"Round 'em up by tomorrow and get them moving."

"What about those two?" growled Merle. "Let me get a few of our best rifle shots and go after them. This is your chance to put the last of the Rustons six feet under."

"Don't be a fool. That man Colbry is a killer. You can see it in his eyes. And what if he kills you? Then I am implicated. And Mackey couldn't help, if that happened. Not his jurisdiction. No, it would be the Texas Rangers coming for me. And in case you haven't heard, they always get their man. Don't think, son. Just do what you're told."

Resentful, Merle spun on his heel and marched out of the room..

Laurie was silent for a long time after they put Elmwood behind them and Colbry rode alongside her without saying a word. When at last she did speak, it was an order stated in a matter-of-fact way.

"I want you to round up as many of our hands as you think you need and go find our missing cattle."

"They may be on their way to Mexico by now. If not, they soon will be."

"Then go after them. Bring them back."

Colbry nodded.

"And don't go and get yourself killed," she added. "Because you have another job when you get back."

"What might that be?

"You need to give us an heir."

He grinned. "Yes, ma'am. Would be my pleasure."

Two mornings later, Colbry woke early. He'd had trouble sleeping in spite of the long, passionate and exhausting lovemaking that he and Laurie had engaged in that night. He rose without waking her, threw on his clothes, and went downstairs. He checked his Schofield, counted the bullets in his gun belt, then checked his Sharps 50-70 carbine. Before he walked out the door he paused to scan the big living room, aware that there was a chance that he wouldn't return. It was an experience he'd had a number of times in his violent life, and it was not going to stop him from doing what needed to be done. Laurie was depending on him. If Faulkner succeeded in profiting from cattle he had stolen from her, he would be emboldened to continue rustling. Then the Rocking Chair Ranch was at risk, because Laurie needed good money to realize her dream.

When he stepped out into the courtyard he was pleased to see Burr Welkin, Emil Canfield, and the six other cowboys he had hand-picked to accompany him. His choices had been made because in months past he had learned a lot about them, and knew which ones were good shots and who'd had experiences fighting other men. More than half of the Rocking Chair crew had fought in the War Between the States. One had been a shotgunner for an express company. Another had been a deputy sheriff for a couple of years. They had their horses with them, and Alonso was moving through them, handing each man a cloth sack containing enough hardtack and salt pork for ten days if carefully rationed. Burr had saddled Boots for him.

"The men we're after are Elmswood cowboys who stole Rocking Chair beeves," said Colbry. "Not sure how much of a head start they have but we will pick up their trail and travel fast. If we have some luck we'll only have to deal with them. They may be meeting up with the Comancheros to sell our cattle. Even so, we're still getting those cattle back. So it will be a hard ride and most likely a hard fight, and for that reason I want to give you boys one last chance to change your mind. I won't hold it against you, if you do. Men are going to die."

They exchanged glances, and some of them spoke up to declare they were ready to ride with him. No one backed out. Colbry gave the tenderfoot Emil Caulfield a long look. Emil noticed and shifted his stance nervously.

"I want to come along, boss," said Emil, his eyes pleading.

Colbry thought it over. He felt protective when it came to the greenhorn, but he realized that if he refused to let Emil come along it would change the way the other cowboys treated the kid from then on. At that precise moment, Burr brought Boots to Colbry and handed over the rein leather.

"We're with you, boss," he said.

"Don't call me that."

"If you didn't want to be called boss, maybe you shouldn't have gotten married. That broke a few bunkhouse hearts, I'll have you know." Burr grinned. "But this ranch belongs to you and your wife now."

Colbry took the reins, put boot to stirrup and mounted the buckskin. "It belongs to all of us." He looked directly at the hopeful Emil Caulfield. "Everybody mount up."

Emil gave a whoop that made a couple of the other men chuckle. Then they climbed into their saddles and followed Colbry out of the courtyard. As he led the way he glanced up at the bedroom window and, sure enough, Laurie was standing there, still clad in her nightclothes, gazing down at him. She raised a hand and he touched the brim of his hat before passing through the gate.

CHAPTER FOURTEEN

They made good progress on the first day, crossing Rattlesnake Flats and then headed west by south. Colbry had decided to skirt the western boundary of the Elmswood range. camping by a spring-fed pond that Burr Welkin knew about. He knew that it would likely put his crew further behind their prey, but decided that crossing onto Faulkner's land was not only unnecessary but risky. If Faulkner was moving the stolen cattle to the border he would cross the boundary of his own ranch eventually, so it was just a matter of time before Colbry found their tracks. It would be impossible to hide the passage of so many cattle. They camped that first night by a spring-fed pond that Burr Welkin knew about.

Late in the second day they found the trail of the cattle Faulkner was sending to the border. It wasn't possible to get a good count of the beeves but Colbry figured there were at least a couple hundred, and by studying the tracks of the shod horses accompanying the herd, he estimated that there were eight drovers.

The pursuit was hard on both men and horses. Colbry had some experience in chasing a hostile force thanks to his years working as a scout for the army in Apacheria, and knew how to cover ground quickly without overtaxing men or mounts. The days were hot and dusty, the grasslands seared a rusty color, as it didn't rain much this time of year. and they rode from early morning until the sun went down, with a short break around midday when they found a copse of trees large enough to give them a little shade, or a spring or creek of water, or both. He constantly changed the pace, depending on the difficulty of the terrain and the hour of the day.

From the talk around the campfires Colbry determined that the Comancheros were located on the other side of the Rio Grande a half day's ride southeast of the Texas town of Del Rio. The Spanish had built a small settlement there at least fifty yards ago, on the north bank of the river. Texans had moved in after Texas achieved statehood in 1846. As for the Comancheros, they maintained a settlement further up the Rio Grande. They were Mexican traders, and had existed since the Pecos Pueblo Treaty eighty years ago. That treaty had ended a decades-old conflict between the Indians and Mexicans living across the river after an army of five hundred men handed the Comanches a serious defeat.

Since then the Comancheros had profited by trading with the Comanches as well as Pueblos and other tribes along the southern border of the United States. There were several Comanchero strongholds to the west, and it was rumored that there was another up in the largely unpopulated Texas Panhandle. They traded in everything that could bring them profit, including arms and women. And they would trade cattle, since many of the tribes were having increasing difficulty finding enough wild game to hunt. There were white men and even some blacks, most of whom were runaway slaves. All of them were cutthroats.

They were on the eastern edge of Comanche country now, so Colbry kept a flank rider a hundred yards west of the main column who kept an eye peeled for trouble while remaining in view of his companions as much as possible. The terrain gradually changed, and by the third day they had put the heat-stunted oaks and shortgrass of the hill country behind them and had begun to cross a flat desert that shimmered in the distance. It was even hotter now and Colbry shortened the days on the backside by an hour. It wouldn't do to push the men or their horses to the limit in the searing heat of a South Texas summer. The one consolation was that they were still gaining on their objective, and he scanned the southern horizon for the telltale cloud of dust that would reveal the herd's presence.

Seven days later they could see that cloud. By Colbry's estimation they were no more than three days from the Rio Grande – and the Comancheros. It seemed to him that the best course of action was to try to intercept the herd before Faulkner's rustlers reached their destination. But it wouldn't do to stampede the herd. How to prevent that? He could think of only one way and informed his crew that night.

They rode as hard as they could the following day. That night, instead of making camp, they waited until the moon was well up in the clear, star-spangled sky, checking their weapons and ammunition and eating a quick supper of jerky and hard tack before getting back in the saddle and riding south.

It wasn't hard to locate their target. The herd couldn't be missed and the rustlers' night camp was easy enough to find. The Rocking Chair crew left their horses some two hundred yards away in a shallow ravine, their long rifles still in their saddle scabbards, with two men staying behind to await Colbry's summons. Then the rest crept closer to the camp. When Colbry heard voices he paused behind some brush, signaled his six cowboys to wait, then crawled closer. He had learned the hard way to move as soundlessly as an

Apache and before long was looking into the camp from just twenty feet away.

He counted seven Elmswood rustlers. Some were already in their blankets, while three had hunkered down next to a small cook fire built in a shallow hole dug into the ground. One was smoking a pipe. A second was puffing on a cheroot. A third was at a wagon carrying several lashed-down barrels of water and some gunny sacks filled with provisions. They were talking softly, and Colbry couldn't make out all the words they spoke but occasionally one or more of the men chuckled.

Colbry crawled back to the waiting Rocking Chair crew and gave his orders without saying a word, indicating how far away the camp was by pointing in its direction and holding up fingers to indicate how many men were in it. Then he pointed to four of the Rocking Chair cowboys, including Burr, to circle around the camp. The other four men, including Caulfield, followed him, creeping as silently as wraiths back to the spot where he had laid eyes on their prey.

When they emerged from the brush and into the weak, flickering throw of the fire's meager light, Colbry had his Schofield pistol in hand, hammer back, so that when two of the rustlers chewing the fat around the dying fire scrambled to their feet, pulling the smoke wagons from their side holsters, he shot one of them in the right shoulder. His target spun and dropped to the ground, the pistol slipping out of his grasp. Colbry shouted at the others to drop their guns. Burr and the other cowboys burst into view on the far side of the camp. One of the rustlers came out of his blankets with rifle in hand and was gunned down.

For a handful of breathless seconds rustlers and cowboys faced off, and Colbry shouted "Drop your iron!" Beyond the camp he heard the nearby herd stirring and realized if there was a shootout in the offing the cattle could stampede. It would be one hell of a job trying to round them all up. He took a step forward and extended his gun arm to point the Schofield at the chest of one of the rustlers who seemed conflicted when it came to following the command. "Point that at me and you'll die," he warned, and saw in the other's expression that he wasn't going to take the chance, and let the pistol slip out of his grasp as he raised his hands.

Colbry performed a quick head-count and realized one rustler was missing. He assumed the man was night-riding around the herd, and there was no doubt that this man would have heard the gunfire. Since he hadn't returned to the night camp to investigate the shooting, he was most likely headed for the closest safe haven. The Comanchero town.

The Rocking Chair men disarmed their prisoners and thoroughly checked blankets and panniers for any other weapons, and then commenced tying up Faulkner's men, checking each one thoroughly for knives or concealed pistols. Colbry picked up one of the knives from a pile of confiscated weapons and cut the tether rope to which the rustlers' horses had been tied and shooed them away. Then he turned to Burl.

"Leave the prisoners. Take their guns. Start the herd for home. Two of you can stay behind and cut these boys loose tomorrow. They can have a knife and a canteen. Leave their horses a day's travel north of here."

"What about you?"

"I have to catch the night guard before he gets to the river." said Colbry. He turned to address the Elmswood cowboys.

"When you find your horses, I suggest you go home. If you come after the herd, we'll gun you down."

Some of the Elmswood men nodded. Others looked away.

Colbry strode through the brush to the spot where they had left their horses. He pulled the reins of his buckskin off the tether rope and climbed into the saddle, then kicked Boots into a leaping start, heading south. The night guard had a good head start, at least a half-mile by now, he reckoned, so he put Boots into a gallop along the side of the herd. Startled cows bellowed and the herd began to move away from him as he thundered past. Once he was beyond it he searched the horizon to the south. After an anxious moment he spotted a black form popping up and then merging again with the darker mass of the terrain. It had to be the night guard, and he was riding hell-for-leather. Colbry kept goading Boots to go faster, bending forward over the horse's neck. There was a risk of a stumble or worse, if the buckskin happened to put a hoof in a gopher hole, but he had to risk it. If the man he was pursuing reached the river and then the Comancheros there would be hell to pay. He didn't look back, knowing that he could rely on Burl and the other Rocking Chair cowboys to round up the herd and get it moving north.

Boots was surefooted, had a lot of stamina, and could run like the wind. But in the night shadows Colbry had a difficult time keeping track of his prey. The terrain was dark and treacherous. More than once the ground seemed to disappear beneath Boot's hooves and they landed hard in a ravine or wallow, knocking the wind out of Colbry. But neither horse nor man let up. Now and then he caught a glimpse of the herd guard outlined against the sky, but just as often the ground seemed to swallow him up as he went down into low spot.

By the position of the moon, Colbry calculated that an hour had passed when he saw the dark barricade of a long low ridge up ahead, and he lost sight of the other rider altogether for a few moments. Then the man was briefly silhouetted on the rim of the ledge. Boots charged resolutely up the slope. At the top, Colbry reined him in. The buckskin's barrel was heaving under his legs.

There was no way he was going to catch the rider that night.

He checked Boots and stroked the buckskin's sweat-drenched neck. By his calculations the Rio Grande was at least several long days away. Catching the rustler that night had been a longshot, and now it was an impossibility. He would have to track the rider, and he needed daylight to do that.

Colbry had no trouble tracking the Elmwood rider the next three days. The man headed south by west instead of circling around to head back to inform Barrett Faulkner that the herd had been lost. He figured that the only reason his prey was doing that was to inform the Comancheros, perhaps hoping that they would cross the border and recover the herd, which they could catch up to before it reached the Rocking Chair ranch if they rode hell for leather.

He knew what Boots could do, and believed it highly likely he was riding the better mount, and as the days passed the tracks proved him right, as the sign he followed became steadily fresher, so that when he woke up on the third day he knew he would likely catch up before sundown. In the late afternoon of a hellishly hot day, he finally spotted the rider he was chasing, and by the time the sun was melting into a hellish red and orange mass on the western horizon, he spotted a river off to the south, the water capturing the last of the sunlight. It had to be the Rio Grande. As he had no idea exactly where the Comanchero town was located but knew he didn't want to take on fifty or more cutthroats, Colbry kicked Boots into a stretched-out gallop. He had to prevent the herd guard from crossing the river.

For a few minutes he couldn't locate his prey. Then he saw a lone rider galloping westward along the riverbank. A minute later, as the gloom of dusk began darkening the land, he saw a little burst of flame and heard the distinctive and chilling sound of a bullet buzzing past his head.

His initial instinct was to draw the Sharps long gun from its boot and return fire, but common sense kicked in and he urged Boots forward, riding hell for leather down the slope to the flats and kicking the buckskin into a stretched-out run again. He saw a shadowy figure highlighted by the wide river, which now looked like blue velvet as the sunset faded into night. The man was riding from his left to his right, and a hundred or so yards away. Colbry threw a quick glance up the river and saw the glimmer of torchlight on the northern bank of the Rio Grande and another directly across the wide river on the southern. This made him wonder if the Comanchero town was very close. The man he was pursuing had turned to race along the river on this side, making for the torches. Colbry assumed they marked a safe crossing, since this river was notorious for its quicksand.

He steered Boots in the direction of the torches and by the time the other man was about to reach them he was close enough to take a shot. He checked the buckskin hard, and was out of the saddle and letting go of the reins before his horse had fully stopped. He took one step away from Boots, whipped the butt of the Sharps to his shoulder and drew a bead on his target, just as the latter reached the torches and without slowing his horse, turned it into the shallows. Colbry took a deep breath, exhaled half of it, then fired.

The rustler was knocked off his horse and tumbled with a splash into the water. His horse raced across the river and disappeared into some brush.

Colbry was back in the saddle and on the move as soon as his target fell. He kept Boots at a canter, peering into the shadows, wondering if the crossing was guarded. But by the time he had reached the body in the shallows, easy to spot in the throw of the torchlight, he was pretty sure the man was dead. But he needed to be sure.

The Sharps secured in its boot, his horse's reins clenched in his left hand, he waded into the river, knelt beside the dead man and pushed him over on his back. He recognized the face. He was dead, shot through the upper body. The 50-70 fired a 450-grain bullet that was capable of going right through an adult buffalo. The entry hole in the rustler's right side was about the size of a Liberty Double Eagle. It had made his left side a mangled, bloody mess.

It was Merle, Faulkner's son.

Colbry didn't linger long in the water. Remounting, he urged Boots into a gallop and headed away from the river, throwing a couple wary glances over his shoulder, wondering if the gunshot had been heard by any badmen on the Mexican side of the Rio Grande. Once over the low ridge, he took a deep breath, reined the buckskin in until it was in a ground-eating canter, and headed north.

Dawn light was turning the eastern sky a pretty shade of blue when he caught up with the stolen herd and the Rocking Chair cowboys. All but the herd guards were sitting or standing around a small fire feasting on hardtack and coffee, with the five glum Elmswood riders, still bound, sitting nearby.

Burl was offering him a tin cup of coffee as soon as he dismounted. Colbry thanked him and took a sip while the other asked him if he had caught up with his prey. Colbry nodded and provided the essential details.

"You were close to the Comanchero town, I reckon, if there were torches lit to mark a safe crossing," mused Burl. "Some of 'em like to travel at night and raid a target right before dawn, when folks are still sleeping. So Faulkner's men were going to sell our beeves to those cutthroats. I hear tell there might be a hundred men in that Godforsaken town. And that's not counting women and children. It's said they just took it over about a century ago. A big bad bunch of outlaws that even the Mexican soldiers are afraid of. They are the most bloodthirsty renegades you'll ever meet. French vide poches, Mexican bandoleros and American outlaws. They have a code of law that is as bloody and heartless as you can imagine. But then I guess they have to, considering that they're the most lawless bunch of robbers, gun sharps, cutthroats that you will ever meet. Even the Comanches and, further west, the Apaches, try to get along with them 'cause to do otherwise is flirting with death and the trade was good. Makes sense they're in the market for beef. Some of them have wives and children. And there are more harlots than you could find in the biggest gold strike camp in the Sierra Madre. It's a good thing you didn't run into any of 'em."

Colbry was drinking the coffee eagerly. He was weary and saddle sore after the arduous night ride, and he had a whole week in the saddle ahead of him. But he was used to this harsh regimen, and the Arbuckle's gave him much-needed energy. "Let's get the herd moving," he suggested. "The Comancheros sound like a bunch I'd rather not meet right now."

"What about Faulkner's men?"

"Saw no sign of them on the way back. I reckon they picked up their horses and made for home. There's one more thing, Burl. The last rustler I shot was Merle Faulkner."

Burl muttered a curse under his breath, then said, "There's going to be hell to pay."

A quarter-hour later the Rocking Chair crew were in the saddle and pushing the herd north. The Comancheros found them that afternoon.

The Comancheros appeared late in the morning of the second day. Colbry had seen the cloud of dust on the southern horizon early in the morning, but wasn't sure at first if it was a large group of riders or a dust devil, a kind of desert tornado. He had seen twenty seven dust devils in one day of travel while scouting for the army in Apacheria. But when this cloud of dust persisted and became bigger, he realized it was a sizable group of riders, a group that was following the herd. It was possible that the Elmswood rustlers had tracked down their horses and were now hot on the trail, but they were unarmed so he doubted that. It was also possible that Merle's body had been discovered by the Comancheros, that they knew him as Barrett Faulkner's son, had probably done business with him before since the elder Faulkner didn't strike Colbry as a man who would ride the range. The Comancheros were after Rocking Chair cattle, and Colbry figured they were out to teach him and his companions a lesson, because they couldn't afford to let others thwart their plans and get away with it.

Burr Welken was one of the flank riders and Colbry rode over to him and put Boots alongside the cowboy's pony.

"I guess you've seen the dust?"

"Yep. Looks like a bunch of 'em."

"No way to know how many but I'm willing to bet that we'll be outnumbered."

Burr was wearing his bandana over the lower half of his face so he didn't inhale all the dust that the cattle were kicking up. Colbry couldn't see Burr's wolfish grin but he saw it in the man's eyes. "You reckon?"

"No way to know how many."

"Oh, I wouldn't say more than five, maybe six, hombres for each one of us."

Colbry scanned the desert flats. There were a couple of low bluffs far to the west, a landmark he had used on the ride south. "If I remember right, there's a dry river bed a few miles ahead. A few men can stay with the herd and keep it moving. The rest of us will hunker down there and hope to buy them some time. If they get past us those men can leave the herd and ride hell for leather north. I'd feel better if you were one of them."

Burr snorted. "Not a chance."

They rode along for a minute or two before Burr started to chuckle. "For the past twenty years or so I've been thinking I should write a will. Not that I have much to leave anyone." He looked earnestly across at Colbry. "Do me a favor and make Emil one of those that stick with the herd."

"He won't cotton to that."

Burr shrugged. "Got to admit, I think of him as the son I never had."

Colbry nodded. "I don't think whoever's chasing us will want to pay too high of a price for a handful of scalps. It's just business for them. We stand a chance, Burr. If we make it too expensive for them, they might call it off."

"We'll know before long."

Colbry extended his hand. "Good luck."

He picked three of the ranch hands to proceed with the herd, one of them being Emil Caulfield. Naturally, all of them objected to not being picked to take a stand against their pursuers. Colbry listened to their entreaties and then smiled and said, "Just do it for Laurie."

When they reached the driver river bed, Colbry and the five cowboys he had selected to stand with him joined him on the edge of the embankment and watched the herd slowly continuing north. No one said a word. Colbry grimly calculated their chances of stopping the Comancheros as slim to none. There was no way of knowing how many there were, but it was a sure bet that it wouldn't be a fair fight, which meant it was possible, maybe even likely, that he would be leading Burl and the cowboys to their deaths. He couldn't avoid thinking about Laurie. If she could, she would tell him to forget about the herd and save his life and the lives of her men. But that would be the end of her dreams. You couldn't let a thief get away with stealing from you, because they would always come back for more. Barrett Faulkner would be emboldened to steal more cattle, or worse, attack the Rocking Chair to drive her away.

"Come on," said Colbry. He led Boots down into the ravine and the others followed suit. He instructed the cowboys to separate themselves by ten strides, with Burl taking the other end of the line. Then he hitched Boots to a heavy rock and took every cartridge he had in his saddlebags for both the Sharps and his pistol, as well as his canteen, and marked his spot with these items before walking down the line and calmly imparting some advice, bending now and then to gather up some bone-dry branches, and, when he had a dozen, sat on his heels, stacked them like a teepee. He made sure the man closest to it had a strike anywhere match and told him to start the deadwood burning once the shooting started. Colbry untied a branding iron from his saddle and placed the business end of the iron on top of the branches.

"Shoot their horses first!" He shouted. "If any of them get among us, use your side gun to take 'em down. If you're hit, slap hot iron on the wound to cauterize it and get back in the fight. Make sure you have your canteen with you. This fight could take five minutes or five hours."

One of the cowboys asked him the question he dreaded most. "Do we stand a chance, Mr. Colbry?"

"And long as you're alive you have a chance."

When he returned to his spot he indulged in a short drink from his canteen and then crawled up the bank of the draw and peered over the edge and estimated that the pursuers were no more than a mile away. He couldn't make out the horses or riders for a little while longer, but when he did he noticed they were riding at the gallop. Seconds later one of the cowboys fired a shot.

"Hold your fire until you can be sure to hit something!" barked Colbry, loud enough for the others to hear him.

The single gunshot didn't unnerve the Comancheros. They came on, hell for leather, and gradually Colbry could hear some of them whooping and hollering. A short time later a few began to fire. He saw a couple of puffs of sand kicked up well short of the river bed, and again called out to his compadres to hold their fire. Then he heard a round whistling overhead. The Comancheros were in range. He bellowed, "Cut 'em down!"

He drew a bead on the nearest rider, less than a hundred yards away, and with a twinge of regret brought down the cutthroat's mount. The man was catapulted into the air and landed clumsily. Colbry brought down a second horse, and then noticed the first man was struggling to get to his feet, dazed or injured or both. Colbry shot him dead. The rest of the Rocking Chair hands were firing as fast as they could, and all along the attacking line Comancheros and their horses were falling.

The wings of the line of attack plunged down into the river bed on either side of the Rocking Chair cowboys, and Colbry found himself flanked by a half-dozen horsemen. He lunged to his feet, crouching, and drew the Schofield pistol. He aimed at the Comancheros who were trying to check and turn their horses and at the same time fire their guns at him. He shot one, a swarthy Mexican, out of his saddle, hitting him square in the chest. The Mexican was dead before he slid sideways out of his saddle. Then he winged a burly Comanchero in the left shoulder, whose bullet screamed past Colbry's head. Colbry flinched, then had to roll out from under the hooves of the man's rearing horse. He came up on one knee and with the next shot knocked a third rider off his saddle.

By now the Rocking Chair hands were shooting at the Comancheros who had reached the dry river bank. Colbry threw a quick glance behind him. his cowboys. Dead or just wounded men and horses littered the ground, and the dust was so thick he couldn't distinguish friend from foe. In that instant the horse of the man he had winged went down, pinning its rider. Colbry lunged over the carcass of the horse at the rider, whose leg was pinned under his mount, knocking the man's gun arm aside even as his gun was triggered, and then pistol-whipped the Comanchero mercilessly with the Schofield, cracking his skull. The Comanchero went limp and Colbry rolled to his right and emptied his pistol into another foe. Two of his bullets hit the target dead center, and the man was gone when he somersaulted over the back of his pony. Still on the ground beside the dead horse and rider, he fired the last round in the Schofield straight up at a black man, bandoleros draped across his bare chest, who was shooting at the Rocking Chair cowboys further down the river bed. The man pulled on rein leather as he died, causing his horse to rear, and Colbry rolled desperately away, trying to avoid the animal's flailing hooves as the animal went down on its side. Then its rider, breathing his last, loosened his grip on the reins and the horse got up, kicking wildly, and Colbry scrambled a little further away.

Suddenly the din of battle lessened. Colbry peered through the dust that partially obscured the men, living and dead, in the dry river bed. He spotted one mounted man aiming his gun at nearly point-blank range at a Rocking Chair cowboy. He got the shot off and the cowboy spun and fell, a second or two before Colbry dived for his Spencer, dug a 50-70 cartridge out of his belt, loaded the single-shot rifle, and fired. The bullet struck the Comanchero squarely in the back and he fell sideways out of his saddle, dead before he hit the ground.

Suddenly the Comancheros were gone, galloping southward, kicking up a cloud of dust and dirt that obscured the view of a few cowboys who were on their feet and still shooting.

Somewhat dazed and breathing hard, his ears ringing, Colbry lay among the carcasses of men and horses and reloaded his pistol. Then he got to feet, steadied himself, and took stock of the situation. A pall of dust and gun smoke, slowly dissipating, hung in the hot, still air over the battleground. He stumbled a bit as he walked down the river bed, anxious to check on his men. One man was on his feet, warily looking southward in the direction of the Comanchero retreat. Another was walking through the pile of dead or dying men and mounts, killing a mortally wounded enemy here and ending the suffering of a gut shot horse there.

But Colbry didn't see Burr Welken. Anxiety shot through him. He called his friend's name. Then again. Someone shouted, "He's over here!" and Colbry picked his way through the carnage with a growing sense of dread. He saw a cowboy down on one knee and beckoning to him, then gently rolling Burl onto his back.

"Afraid he's met his Maker, sir," said the cowboy, struggling to maintain his composure. He knuckled his eye and muttered, "Damn dust." Colbry doubted it was really the dust hanging over the scene of battle that was making the man's eyes moisten.

Colbry dropped wearily to his knees beside the body of his friend. Burr's pistol was still clenched in his hand, and Colbry gently pried open the fingers, picked up the gun and stuck it under his own belt. Then he put a hand on the morose cowboy's shoulder. The young cowboy was wiping at his eyes. Two more Rocking Chair hands came closer to loom over them. A gunshot made everyone jump. The man walking through the carnage in the river bed had put a dying Comanchero out of his misery.

All the energy seemed to drain right out of Colbry's body. Beyond the river bank to the south, dead men and horses littered the ground. He heard a horse whinny plaintively from out there, and the cowboy who had been standing watch walked over to him.

"Someone needs to go out there and put down the horses that are suffering," said the cowboy, angrily. "And rid this world of any damned Comanchero that's still breathing. I got nary a scratch." He was astonished at his good fortune, and looked skyward. "Thank you, Lord. I reckon I can do it."

Colbry nodded and thanked him. The cowboy who had checked the bodies in the river bed came up and slumped to the ground near Burl's body and informed Colbry that he had counted nine dead Comancheros.

A gunshot rang out. Both of them flinched. Colbry's nerves were frayed, and he knew the same was true of the other Rocking Chair cowboy. Then they realized it was their compadre, out beyond the river bed, putting a man or a horse out of its misery. The man who had done the count gazed morosely at Burl Welken.

"Sure am going to miss him," he sighed.

They buried Burr and the other dead Rocking Chair cowboys about a hundred paces north of the carnage in and around the dry river bed, in a spot where some blackbush and a few scrawny mesquites formed a small thicket. The bodies were wrapped in blankets and the few oilskin tarps that some of the hands carried to make shelter. They dug the graves with knives and tin plates. It was hard and sweaty work in the heat of midday, but they buried their friends deep then piled rocks on top of the graves. Shallow graves in a land of coyotes wouldn't suffice. They didn't make makeshift crosses. In a month or maybe less depending on the weather and the wind, the mounds of dirt would be flattened, the gravesites virtually indistinguishable from the rest of the desert plains. But Colbry knew he could find the thicket again and the others trusted that he would.

When the dead had been laid to rest, the cowboys turned to Colbry to say a prayer. He said the only one he knew.

"Our Father who art in heaven, hallowed be thy name. Thy kingdom come. Thy will be done on earth as it is in heaven. Give us this day our daily bread and forgive our trespasses, as we forgive those who trespass against us, and lead us not into temptation, but deliver us from evil. For thine is the kingdom, the power, and the glory. Amen."

"Amen," said the others.

"I want you to know," said Colbry, "that I aim on coming back here with a wagon. These men died for the Rocking Chair ranch and they deserve to lay in rest there." He was confident that he could find the thicket again and the others trusted that he would.

"I'm coming back with you," said one cowboy.

"Me, too," said another.

"Count me in," said a third.

Colbry slapped his dust-caked hat on his leg and then planted it firmly on his head. "Let's catch up with the herd. When we do, I am riding on ahead." He wasn't sure how long it would take for Faulkner to hear about his son, but it was a pretty safe bet that when he found out there would be hell to pay.

He turned to climb into the saddle of his buckskin, standing ground-hitched a few steps away, and stashed Burr Welken's pistol in a saddlebag, intent on presenting it to Emil Caulfield. He grimaced as he urged Boots into a canter. Every stride of the horse beneath him sent fresh pain from his gunshot wound lancing through his arm and shoulder. The others climbed into their saddles and followed, heads hanging and heavy of heart.

CHAPTER FIFTEEN

When Trace Simmons answered a summons from Barrett Faulkner he was ushered into the Elmwood library by one of the Mexican girls and was shocked by the appearance of his boss. Faulkner was slumped in a chair, pale and distraught. The hand holding a shot glass of whiskey was shaking. He was staring at the floor and didn't seem aware that Simmons had come into the room.

Simmons cleared his throat and Faulkner raised his head and looked around but said nothing.

"You wanted to see me?" asked Simmons.

"My son … Merle is dead."

Simmons nodded. The men Faulkner had sent to push the stolen cattle south to Mexico had returned with the news. They hadn't known the name of the Rocking Chair man who had gone after Merle, but they had been present when that man returned with news of Merle's death.

"I'm sorry to hear that, boss," said Simmons. It was a lie. He had already calculated that Merle's death might be a break for him. After all, Merle had been the foreman of the Elmwood ranch. Someone would have to take his place, and Simmons had hoped that today's summons meant that Faulkner was going to name him as the new foreman.

Barrett Faulkner stood up, a bit wobbly. Then he hurled his glass at one bookcase-lined wall, with such force that the glass shattered. He turned to face Simmons, and his gaunt face was twisted in a rictus of hot rage.

"I want you to kill Laurie Ruston's thoroughbred."

Simmons was caught off guard. He hadn't expected this. "From what the men say, it was Colbry who killed your son. Why don't I bring you his head."

Faulkner took two steps closer. He was wobbly, off-balance, and Simmons thought maybe he had too much brandy. He stabbed a bony finger at Simmons' chest. "You do what I tell you and do it now. But that bastard is out on the range somewhere, bringing those damned Rocking Chair beeves home. I want that horse dead now! You hear me?"

Simmons clenched his teeth. He didn't like being talked to that way. "Yes, sir."

As he turned and left the manor a cold smile curled his mouth.

That same day Colbry arrived at the Rocking Chair ranch house. He was tired and sore when he stepped down out of the buckskin's saddle, but his weariness was forgotten the instant Laurie came bursting out of the door of the main room, running into his arms, draping hers over his shoulders and smothering him with kisses.

"I was so worried," she gasped, when she came up for air, her arms loosening around his neck and wrapping around his midsection as she rested her head on his chest.

Alonso showed up, grinning happily from ear to ear. "Gracias a Dios!" he exclaimed, and stepped up to take the buckskin's reins. "I will take good care of him, senor."

Colbry pulled his Spencer rifle out of its boot, thanked the old Mexican, and followed his wife inside. Laurie sat with him near the stone hearth. He actually sighed with relief as he settled down in an upholstered chair.

"Saddle sore?" she asked, with a sympathetic smile.

"I must be getting old."

"We could spend the next few days in bed," she murmured, with a saucy curl to her lips. Then her smile faded and she read Colbry's expression. "What's wrong?"

"I have bad news. Burr is dead."

Stunned, Laurie stared at him, then swiped at eyes that suddenly glistened with tears. She stood up and stepped up to the hearth, staring at the ashes of the fire that had last burned within it.

"Tell me," she said softly, tears streaking her cheeks. "Tell me everything that happened."

Colbry did, without embellishment, and finished with, "He was a good man. Best man I ever knew."

Laurie choked back a sob, swiped at her eyes and turned to face him.

"I want you to bring his body back here. The other cowboys that died that day, as well. I want them to rest in peace here with us"

Colbry nodded. "I will. But not now."

"And why not?"

"Because I shot and killed Merle Faulkner."

Laurie turned around to face him, her eyes wide.

"It may be that Faulkner hasn't gotten word of it yet," continued Colbry. "But if not, he will soon."

Laurie sighed. "And so we'll have a range war. More men will die."

"Could be. But until we know, I am staying here."

She stepped into his arms and held him tightly while she quietly sobbed.

Trace Simmons waited a couple of miles away from the Rocking Chair ranch buildings until after the moon had set, about an hour before dawn light would begin to suffuse the eastern sky. He knew that at dawn or shortly thereafter the ranch would begin to come to life, and figured now, when it was darkest, he could make it to the stables and find Beholden without running into anyone.

He rode hard until he was a few hundred yards away from his destination, then used the terrain he knew so well and avoided skylining himself by coming in from the southwest. Only the starlight could illuminate him then, and that wasn't enough even if there was a lookout. More than a hundred yards away from the ranch house he hitched his horse to some deadwood and went the rest of the way on foot. He took his rifle and saddlebags with him, the latter slung over his shoulder so that he would have both hands free in the event he had to fire the rifle.

No matter how he killed Beholden, the horse would not die quietly. But Simmons didn't plan to kill the thoroughbred. Barrett Faulkner wanted vengeance, but he wanted the horse. Faulkner didn't care if he came back alive. What would that bastard care if he made off with the thoroughbred rather than killed it, reasoned Simmons. Either way, Laurie Ruston's dream would be ruined. He untied the lariat from his saddle rig and made a slip-knot noose on one end.

Simmons wasn't sure what he would do with such a splendid animal. Maybe keep it for himself. Maybe sell it for a pretty penny in Austin or San Antonio. He had no idea how much such a horse would bring, but the amount wouldn't be anything to sneeze at. He would have more money in his poke than he had ever had in his life. What he was sure of was that he hated being just another hired hand. As John Ruston's foreman he had been able to give the hard work to the cowboys. They had known he was a shirker but he hadn't cared what they'd said about him.

As he drew closer he noticed that, as usual, the big gate to the main house was closed. In his experience as foreman of the Rocking Chair, that had almost always been the case. He stayed in the night shadow of the large structure and made it to the corner from whence he could see the stable, forty yards away. Beyond it was the bunkhouse and the corrals. Nothing was stirring. Even the chickens that Alonso raised out the back door of the kitchen in the big house wouldn't be stirring for a little while longer. He catfooted it to the front of the stable, then used that structure's night shadow to work his way silently around to the side, where a door was located. He took one more look around then pulled the rope latch slowly, lifting the bar out of its cradle on the other side. The door's hinges creaked just a bit. A horse whickered. He slipped inside and paused, letting his eyes adjust to the darkness.

The stable was full of horses, but it didn't take long for him to find Beholden. The thoroughbred stood apart from the cow ponies. A few horses whickered as he passed their stalls, and one even snorted and began circling. Simmons knew he had to be quick. He worked the latch on Beholden's stall. The stallion eyed him and circled to the back of the stall, watching balefully. Simmons grinned.

"You're coming with me, boy," he whispered. "You're my ticket to good times."

"No, he isn't."

Simmons froze, shoulders hunching, his heart suddenly racing. He recognized the voice.

It was Cord Colbry.

He looked slowly over his shoulder and saw Colbry standing there, just outside. The Schofield pistol was drawn and aimed at him.

"Drop the rope," said Colbry, "then use your left hand to throw away that smoke wagon on your hip."

Simmons realized that Colbry couldn't see the sheathed Bowie knife that rode on the front of his left hip. He let go of the rope and slowly reached across his body to lift the pistol out of its holster and tossed it aside. His head was turned so that he could watch Colbry out of the corner of his eye. He said nothing. There was nothing he could say to explain his presence.

"So you work for Faulkner now," said Colbry. It wasn't a question.

"Not any more. He wanted me to but I decided to take this horse for myself," muttered Simmons. "But I didn't steal him, did I. So I'm not a horse thief."

"No, I figured Faulkner sent you. He paid hired guns to kill Laurie. He turned rustler trying to ruin her. And then he wanted this horse dead to break her."

"He did but I wasn't going to do it!" exclaimed Simmons. He was breathing high and fast. His heart was galloping in his chest. He was losing his nerve. He looked into Colbry's eyes and then away. They were the eyes of a stone cold killer.

"No, you never were," said Colbry quietly. "I figured someone would come for that horse. It was the only play left to Faulkner. He doesn't have the guts to lead his crew and have it out with us face to face, gun to gun. All I had to do was spend a couple of nights out here. I've slept in worse places."

Beholden was becoming more agitated, moving around in his stall, snorting, his long mane flying as he jerked his head up and down.

"Take two steps back and close up that stall or that stallion will kill you before I do."

"You gonna gun me down in cold blood?" asked Simmons, his voice trembling as he did as he was told. He noticed that Colbry didn't seem the least bit nervous. Or angry. He was just very calm, relaxed. "So … what now?"

"This ends one of two ways. Either I turn you over to a U.S. Marshal and you tell him all about Faulkner's war against the Rocking Chair ranch, or you go for that big knife you carry. Personally, I don't care which one you choose."

Simmons lost his nerve then, and his water. "Don't shoot," sighed Simmons, his voice hoarse and shaky. "I'm gonna drop the knife." He used thumb and forefinger to pull the Bowie knife out of its sheath on his left hip and dropped it, then kicked it away.

That night Trace Simmons was tied to a fence post and watched over by Rocking Chair cowboys on two hour shifts. The next morning Colbry hauled him into Lampasas and turned him over to Mackey. He strongly advised the sheriff to keep Simmons locked up until a United States Marshal arrived to take him.

"I'm going over to the telegraph office to send a message to the marshal in Austin. And I'm going to wait there until I get a reply."

"How do you know the marshal will come?"

"Oh, he will. And Simmons better be here or you could lose that badge. Or worse."

There was a glimmer of fear in Mackey's eyes but he tried to mask it with belligerence. "Are you threatening me, Colbry?"

"No. I'm promising you."

Colbry waited a handful of seconds before walking out, disappointed that Mackey hadn't take further issue with his words.

He waited less than an hour at the telegraph office before he received a response from a John Morrison, United States Marshall. He walked back to the sheriff's office, opened the door, made sure that Mackey was sitting at his desk and said. "Marshal will be here in two days." He slammed the door, got on his horse, and rode out of town.

The next morning Colbry left the ranch in the company of Emil Caulfield, who insisted on coming along, and two other Rocking Chair hands. Their mission was to recover the bodies of Burr Welken and the other cowboys who had died in the fight with the Comancheros. Laurie had wanted to come along but Colbry had talked her out of it, recommending that she make the arrangements for a proper burial of the men who had given their lives for the ranch.

The journey was uneventful, and they returned a fortnight later with the bodies wrapped in tarpaulins tied up with rope. The following day, the dead were properly interred in a small cemetery near the ranch buildings, in the shade of a grove of tall live oaks. The Lampasas minister was there to perform the service.

Once it was done, the Rocking Chair cowboys drifted away one by one, until Colbry and Laurie were the only people left. He put his arm around her and held her close until she was ready to go, admiring her for the fact that she had managed not to cry at all. They walked slowly, hand in hand, toward the ranch house. Colbry saw Alonso emerge from the back door and begin to collect eggs from the hens nests nearby.

"Is it over?" asked Laurie. "I mean truly over?"

Colbry said it was.

"I have some news," she said, and suddenly stopped, tugging on his arm until he turned to face her. He looked into her eyes and glimpsed the depth of her love, and it made him forget everything from his past that had haunted him. "While you were away bringing in our dead, I . . . I missed my time."

"What do you mean?"

"I mean I think we're going to have a baby."

He stared at her, speechless and slack-jawed, and she leaned into him, putting her arms around him.

"if it's a baby girl I would like to name her after my mother. If it's a boy, I would like to name him after you father." She squeezed him. "Even though I don't know your father's name."

"Clay."

"Then Clay it is."

Colbry stood there holding her tightly, and wasn't sure how much time passed before he heard a rider coming hell for leather. His first thought was that he had left his guns in the ranch house. But it was a Rocking Chair cowboy, who stopped his cowpony so abruptly that the horse just about sat down, kicking up a cloud of dirt and dust.

"Now what," muttered Colbry.

"Sorry, Miss Ruston," said the cowboy as Laurie coughed a bit until the cloud had moseyed away. "Heard the news in town. Barrett Faulkner is dead. Word is he shot himself. Grieving over the death of his son, some people say." The cowboy pushed his hat back off his forehead and draped arms over his saddle horn. "Or maybe because ol' Trace Simmons might spill the beans about stolen cattle or cozying up with those Comancheros."

Colbry was surprised that he didn't feel relieved. Instead he thought of Merle, lying dead in the shallows of the Rio Grande river. He took off his hat and ran fingers through his hair, then shook his head.

"I should have buried him."

Laurie held his arm tightly against her body and they walked home together.

THE END

About the Author

Jason Manning is a Texas-born author of over fifty published novels, with three children and a life-long interest in history, horses, dogs and guns.

About the Publisher

This book is published on behalf of the author by the Ethan Ellenberg Literary Agency.
https://ethanellenberg.com
Email: agent@ethanellenberg.com
Facebook: https://www.facebook.com/EthanEllenberg LiteraryAgency/